RUTLAND'S CURSE

Roger Carpenter

Pen Press Publishers Ltd

www.roger-carpenter.co.uk

First published in Great Britain by
Pen Press Publishers Ltd
25 Eastern Place
Brighton BN2 1GJ

ISBN 1-905203-13-6

Printed and bound in the UK

A catalogue record of this book is available from
the British Library

Cover design by Jacqueline Abromeit

To Tom, John and Paul - gunners all.

Prologue

SHERPUR FORTRESS, KABUL, AFGHANISTAN, 1879

Peter staggered in a daze to the breach in the wall. The side of his uniform from collar to puttees was splattered with blood, he could feel it wet on his face – freezing in the bitter air. He shook his head to clear his thoughts but the overwhelming screaming was swamping his mind. Hundreds of voices clashing and blending; howling war cries mixed with the screams of the wounded. He clapped his hands over his ears to shut it all out; he wanted it to stop so he could think – just a moment's quiet to let him think but the howling horde kept getting closer. Through the swirling gun smoke raced the religion-crazed Afghan zealots holding their black banners aloft, leading the unstoppable charge across the arid rocky ground towards the weakening defenders.

"Canister! Independent targets!" He shouted out the fire command through the choking dust to both his Bombardiers. In the wild activity they acknowledged his order with a quickly raised hand. Thank God both of them were still unhurt.

He looked up at the firing platform on the wall above him where the 4th Sikhs were loading, firing and dying, amid gun smoke and blood. Hundreds of empty brass cartridges littered the ground at their feet but the hail of bullets fired from their Martini Henry rifles was still not enough. Nearly one third of the Sikh company had fallen while most of the survivors now showed wounds through their torn and bloodstained uniforms. He wiped his smoke-blackened hand across his sweating face.

"Drivers!" He turned and yelled to the men grouped behind him holding the reins of the stolid artillery mules. "All of you! Get spare carbines, down here, between the guns!"

This swarming Ghazi charge was not going to be held by just his two 7 pounder screw guns and the remaining Sikhs but a few extra carbines will help a little. Maybe some reinforcements are on their way. Maybe?

His blood-soaked uniform was slowly drying out in the freezing wintry Afghanistan sun, stiffening the cloth as it caked hard. It was not his own blood but that of some poor Sikh who had taken the full force of the exploding Afghan shell and, in dying, had spread his blood and intestines all over Peter. Enemy bullets were slamming into brick and flesh all around him as the sniping tribesmen fired into the Sherpur fortress in seemingly ever increasing amounts.

He felt a push in his back, and he was jostled aside by a swarm of small, swarthy-skinned men who came running towards the defence position from somewhere behind him. All were dressed in dark green, wearing pillbox hats and carrying Martini Henry rifles. Thank God! Headquarters had seen their trouble and had sent the 2nd Ghurkhas to support the Sikhs. In single files the stocky little men dashed up the stone steps to the firing platform and, kneeling beside the empty embrasures, started to pour an overwhelming storm of bullets into the leading Afghans who were now only fifty yards away.

His two mountain screw guns crashed out their deadly case-shot; once more the gunners threw themselves through the belching smoke to load the burning hot barrel almost before it had settled from the recoil. Feeding, ramming, priming, firing; it seemed endless.

The noise was still deafening but – surely the sounds were gradually changing; the rifle fire seemed much louder than before, while the war cries were fewer. There were certainly fewer bullets howling into the gunners' position and, now with the Ghurkhas support, many more were tearing into the tribesmen.

He crouched down between his two guns on their squat wheels; through the dust and smoke it looked as though the charge was slowing. He could see the bloody heaps that told where the brave mad-crazed front ranks had died, only a few yards from the bullet-pocked fortress walls. The main body of tribesmen, who were not so fervent in their religious zeal, were now lying down firing at the defenders from any available cover, 300 to 400 yards away.

"Left section!" He yelled at the top of his cracking voice. "Shrapnel. 300 yards. Independent targets. Fire."

Number 1 gun banged out its loaded canister of case shot, while Bombardier Farrant on Number 2 gun scrambled to set the fuse on the shrapnel shell before it was loaded into the barrel and rammed home.

"Bombardier Smith! Concentrate your fire on the area by the enemy field gun."

"Right, sir."

"Bombardier Farrant, sweep the area to the front and the left."

Farrant acknowledged the order with a raised arm, and moved the screw gun with the handspike to aim at a concentration of tribesmen protected by rocks and then, standing clear of the wheels, he shouted, "Fire!"

The Number 5, Gunner Murray, pulled the lanyard attached to the friction tube and the 7 pounder slammed its shell into the air.

"Load!" yelled Farrant and turned to fuse the next shell. Gunner Jenks, the Number 2, leapt towards the muzzle with the sponge and rammer.

"Wotcher doin', Jenks?" yelled Farrant, for the gunner was not ramming the shell but slowly walking past the barrel with his arms hanging by his side.

"Get back to yer bleedin' post!" But Jenks was a dead man; the heavy Snider slug from an Afghan rifle had torn through his chest and was now lodged into his spine.

"Tiny!" shouted Farrant. "Get the rammer."

A large broad-shouldered man jumped up from the pile of ready ammunition and grabbed the sponge and rammer. As he worked, his boots stirred up the dust of the desert sand that slowly settled onto the blind, open eyes of 83724 Gunner Jenks.

Through the smoke of the continuous rattle of the rifle fire from the Sikhs and the Ghurkhas, Peter could see the occasional tribesman jerk up and fall back as a heavy Martini Henry slug tore into him. They can't take much more of this, he thought, even with their fanatical bravery they must break soon. But he was wrong.

"'Ere they come again!" yelled Bombardier Smith.

This time a group of thirty warriors rose together and charged towards the breached wall. As Peter started to call to Number 1 gun to fire on them, he saw the cluster slowly disappear as, in twos and threes, they fell to the deadly rifle fire from the infantry lining the walls.

It was at that very moment that the attack failed, when the heart suddenly went out of the rest of Musa Khan's force. Seeing this last charge cut down so swiftly, the remaining tribesmen turned then ran, crawled and dragged themselves away towards the houses in the city. The rifles of the Sikhs and Ghurkhas continued to crack out at the retreating enemy until the groaning wounded and silent dead were all that remained.

"We've done it, sir." Smith flashed a gap-toothed smile across his smoke-blackened face. "That was a tough 'un."

Peter looked across at the bodies of his two Sergeants lying against the wall; one of them was certainly dead. These two men who he had come to rely on, trust and even admire.

"Yes, Bombardier. That was bloody tough – and a bit different from Newport!" The comment drew a few weary smiles from Smith's gun crew.

Now, slowly and wearily, all the gunners stood up from their squat mountain guns and watched, through the clearing smoke as the enemy reached the security of the city buildings. The attack was over – but Peter knew it was not quite finished just yet.

"Left Section," he called out. "five rounds common shell. 900 yards at the houses. Fire."

The exhausted gunners dragged themselves back into position and started loading, ramming and firing to complete the fire order.

As he watched the fall of the shells into the buildings, Peter thought to himself, surely they won't come again; we've had enough. Then he smiled, amused at his own thoughts. Here am I, 2nd Lieutenant Peter Rutland, Royal Artillery, outside Kabul on Christmas Eve 1879 hoping for peace, yet only a short few months ago we were all in England, bored with training and praying for action – somewhere to win glory.

He looked at the smoke-clouded gun site with dead and wounded littered around. Yes this is a lot different from Newport – and before I knew about the Curse.

Chapter 1

NEWPORT 1878

Peter stood on the side of the tree-lined Nant Carn valley in the Cwmbran Hills above Newport. The two 7 pounder screw guns of his section of mountain artillery were positioned a few yards below him, assembled and ready for action while the panting gunners knelt in their fire positions around them. After the exertion of assembling the guns all the men were sweating, even in the cold Welsh drizzle that fogged the air. On this fifth day of the training exercise, they had assembled and dismantled their pieces three times already in various precarious positions on the Welsh hillsides. The gunners waited for a Fire Order – a series of dummy loading and firing – which would give them time to get their breath back.

Peter looked around him through the steady drizzle. He was wet and cold. He smiled to himself as he thought of his discomfort. "I should be bloody miserable."

He had been commissioned only six months ago and had gone straight to the Darlings of the Gunners – the Royal Horse Artillery. Then, after only four months of the glamour of fine horses, ceremonial drills plus being stationed at Woolwich so close to London and female company, came the posting to Newport and the mountain artillery.

The swank and polish of the RHA busbied uniform, riding about on fast moving horses in immaculate condition, was all exchanged for the stub-trailed screw gun that broke into bits and was carried at a walking pace on five mules.

He looked down the hillside at his section where Sergeant Hills, the section sergeant, was the Number 1 of Number 1 gun. Hills the stocky man of Kent built like a squat oak tree, who had in only a few weeks shown his newly acquired section commander that these new long-barrelled screw guns were the cream of the Artillery. Hills who, standing like a ramrod on the drill square at Raglan Barracks, had proudly said. "Screw guns, sir. The finest. 'We goes where wheels can't' is our motto, sir." Hills who, with patient diplomacy and occasional firmness, had taught Peter all the gunners drill for his "beauties". Hills, the father of the section; he trained, encouraged, reprimanded and, when necessary, even consoled the gunners in his section.

Sergeant Williams, the Number 1 of Number 2 gun was Hills' right-hand man. Between them they had forged their gunners, who came from many walks of life, into a single-minded section. Over the past few weeks Peter had become acquainted with the characters, faces and names of all the individual men in his section. Mabbs, the large Cockney whose perpetual industry was avoiding work of any description, and who had a cheeky wit bordering on insubordination. Palmer, the young Kentish lad who seemed incredibly accident prone; if there was blood on a trail it was always Palmer who had a cut hand – and of course there was Powell, the soft-spoken Welshman. But Peter knew that at present as their new section commander, he was still an outsider.

Cupping his hands to his mouth he shouted out the order that the still panting gunners dreaded to hear. "Left Section. Limber up!"

Groaning inwardly the weary men went into their much practised drill. The barrel was lifted off the carriage and unscrewed into its two basic parts. The wheels were detached from the carriage and all sections lifted and attached to the special harness on each of the carrying mules.

With Number 2 gun dismantled, Sergeant Williams shouted the order, "Lift." The gun carriage was hoisted onto the mule harness and settled into position. The right wheel was lifted onto one side of the wheel mule but Palmer and

Hart, the numbers 3 and 7, were on the lower side. They lifted the left wheel up, thought it was firmly on the harness – and let go. The spokes had only missed the carrying hooks by an inch but the wheel dropped to the ground and, with a mind of its own, started to roll down the hill.

"Grab that wheel y' daft buggers," yelled Williams. The two men lunged, and missed, falling in a heap on top of one another.

"Gawd'elp us," moaned Williams. "Go on – chase the bloody thing." The gunners threw themselves after the speeding wheel that seemed able to miss all the obstacles in its path while the chasing men tripped and fell over repeatedly. The rest of the gun crew stood about yelling delight at their mates' predicament.

"Orl right, orl right you lot, shut your row," Bombardier Farrant called out. The catcalls stopped and the remaining gun crew watched the two struggling gunners pulling and rolling the cumbersome wheel back up the slope again.

Farrant turned to his Sergeant and said, "Good job we ain't being shot at."

"Those two'll wish they'd been 'it by a bullet when I've finished with 'em."

From his position above the section Peter watched the incident. It was all part of their training he thought – and mine. Come to think of it, supposing we were being sniped at, what would I do? He looked across the valley; there were plenty of places for a sniper to hide. I'd order the spare gunners and drivers to use their carbines to return fire and… Of course! I'd get Gunner Powell to use his rifle.

Powell was the only man in the Battery who had been given permission to have an Infantry Martini Henry rifle, because shooting was his sport. The Battery Commander, Major Tenet, had allowed Powell to compete at Wimbledon for the Queen's Prize earlier in the year. Powell's shooting on the rifle ranges was amazingly accurate. I would get him to winkle out the snipers with a bullet between the eyes for each one.

Peter looked down at his grimy hands and his soaking wet uniform. The blue serge was now a sodden black, dotted with mud. God I'm a wreck. I never looked like this in the RHA but then I was never so fit, with all the smoking and drinking plus little strenuous exercise. No, I'm a different man, he wearily admitted to himself as he walked down the hillside to his section, and I might be better for it.

"Quiet gentlemen. The Battery Commander would like to address you." Captain Dainby raised his voice above the chatter of conversation at the battery dining table that evening.

Peter looked at the captain, he was a small man in stature but he had an amazing amount of hair on his face. The bushy side-whiskers, not quite meeting at his chin to form an illegal beard, were joined across his face by a large hairy moustache. Douglas Dainby was old for a Captain, the white hair on his face and head told that. When Peter had joined the Battery he had asked the Centre Section Commander, Lieutenant Henry Bulstrode about Dainby.

Henry's reply was not very helpful. "We all think he blotted his copybook some time ago, he's certainly stuck in a rut but madly keen to see action – especially in India. Says he wants to find a Maharaja's jewels to retire on."

Pompous Dainby. Officious Dainby. Peter had already run up against him for a minor transgression that the Captain had enlarged out of all proportions. Peter wondered if Dainby was just knocking a newcomer into line, or if there was a personal grudge.

"Gentlemen. Quiet!" Dainby again ordered, his red face showing through the white whiskers.

Major Tenet raised his hand to still the Captain's rising anger, then he slowly took a sip from his glass of port and drew in smoke from his cigar while silence fell on the table.

Something's up! The Old Man always likes an audience when there is an announcement to make. He's dangling us on a line.

The major leaned forward, the creak of his chair a sudden noise in the now silent room. He gently rolled the ash from his cigar into the silver ashtray on the table in front of him.

"Harrumph," he cleared his throat. Yes there was certainly something big coming. Tim Tailby, the Right Section Commander, and Henry Bulstrode had both had the experience of the Major's benevolent theatricals. They were now all sitting on the edge of their chairs, fully attentive.

"Gentlemen, as you know the North West Frontier of India is always an unsettled area." He paused, possibly for effect.

The North West Frontier! We are going to be posted to India! No wonder the Old Man was being dramatic.

"Quiet, gentlemen, please." Tenet drew on his cigar. "Well, we are not being sent there." He looked around the table through his twinkling eyes at the perplexed faces. "No," he continued. "We are being posted to the Kurram Valley." Again he paused; it was obvious that no one except the Battery Commander knew where the Kurram Valley was.

"Kurram is the gateway to Afghanistan, 100 miles west of Peshawar. A new British Ambassador, Sir Louis Cavagnari, is about to open a new residency in Kabul with the blessing of the present Amir, Yakub Khan. We will be stationed at Kurram just outside Afghanistan to make sure that the Amir keeps to his promises."

To the gunner officers seated at the table, this news was good news. All Victorian military officers craved for foreign posting; hopefully a small war where glory and promotion could be won.

Afghanistan! Peter thought of the pleasure the news would bring to his father who, as Major Arthur Rutland RA (retired) had been in the Afghan war of 1840. A matter of the son following in his father's footsteps.

"The Russians have advanced their frontiers right up through the Hindu Kush to the northern borders of Afghanistan," the Major continued, "but with the Amir friendly to England, plus our military strengths behind him, we will be able to keep the Russians clear of India." Again the Major drew on his cigar, as the seated officers absorbed these facts. Then he reached inside his mess waistcoat and pulled out a piece of paper that he laid on the table.

"Now, gentlemen, for the details. We'll embark on 29th January at the Royal Albert Docks in London, and sail via the Suez Canal to Karachi. Nothing unusual about that but the surprise is the ship we shall sail in. Apparently we are the only military group being sent to Karachi at this time; we will therefore not be travelling on a transport ship but," he paused, with a twinkle in his eye, to draw on his cigar, "we sail as passengers on the P&O liner scheduled for that voyage. Those of you who have had to endure the discomfort of the troopship will be overjoyed that officers will travel as second-class passengers, NCOs and gunners in steerage."

At this news, Tim Tailby beamed his pleasure towards Henry and Peter. A foreign posting – India, Afghanistan – and to travel in style.

"Incidentally," continued the Major, "I've heard that 11/9 mountain battery also with screw guns, who are based at Bombay, have been told to move to Kurram. The GOC wishes to have us both available for any necessary mountain warfare that may be expected.

"Seven days of embarkation leave will start in stages from next week." The Major picked up his glass of port and raised it. "Gentlemen, I propose a toast. To a speedy passage to Karachi – which incidentally should be damned pleasant."

Peter pulled the high collar of his blue Artillery greatcoat around his neck and settled his cap onto his unruly brown hair that was almost too long to be acceptable for the Army.

He watched the frost-covered fields slip by as the trotting horses pulled the family dogcart through the Surrey lanes.

"Good to have you home again, Master Peter," croaked Joby. The perpetual broken-stemmed, clay pipe clenched in his mouth.

"It's good to be home, Joby."

"You'm staying long?"

"No. A few days' leave before posting to foreign parts."

"Ah well, it's the only way for Missus Victorier to keep 'er Empire. You young'uns gotter 'old it tight." He tossed the reins on the horse's back.

"My father fought at Waterloo," he continued in his rural drawl, "an' 'e always said the world would be a better place if old England ruled all of Europe, especially the Frogs."

Peter allowed Joby to prattle on. He had heard the old coachman's stories and imperialistic opinions so often. As the wheels crunched along the high road he felt his love of this part of England. The village of Chellingham lay high up in the North Downs, in an area where long distances can be seen from the few fields that are not closely bounded by large treed copses or tall hedgerows. From the top edge of some of the south-facing fields it was possible to see the countryside of the Sussex Weald, Dalmatian-spotted with small towns and villages. Occasionally the ephemeral smoke-trail from a railway engine joined two of these towns where invisible markets bustled. The view from the north-facing fields only rarely penetrated right into the heart of the City of London, but then the rounded dome of St Paul's Cathedral could be seen rising above the surrounding buildings. The coal-smoke laden air from crowded suburbia generally cloaked this view in winter except for the rare bright frosty days as today.

"'Ere we are then, Master Peter."

With gentle and firm rein control, Joby turned the horses off the village road and down at the knapped flint surface of the drive leading to Chellingham Place.

As the dogcart swung into the gravel courtyard, Peter could see his father standing at the open front door. Obviously the Major had been watching for its approach down the drive.

Peter looked around him before he climbed down. Whenever he had been away for some time he always relished the sight of the old farmhouse.

It was a yeoman farm originally built in the 17th century that had been added to by the Major some ten years ago. The addition of a large sitting room with bedrooms above at one end, plus a large kitchen and servants' rooms at the other made the building long and comparatively narrow. The old house formed one side of a square around the large courtyard with the other two sides made by a line of stables and hay barns plus coach house and groom's quarters. The fourth side of the enclosed area was an old brick wall pierced by a central gateway marked by two large columns on which were hung filigreed wrought iron gates.

"Damned good to see you, my boy," the Major beamed as Peter gave his mother a hug. "Come along inside, you must be frozen."

Peter walked into the beamed hall and pulled off his greatcoat.

"Peter! You beast."

He turned towards the cry, and saw Teressa his twin sister running towards him with outstretched arms.

"Tess," he called. They both hugged each other. "Tess, you're beautiful."

He held her at arm's length. "Has no one proposed to you yet? They must be mad – or is it you've given them all a taste of your temper?"

Tess stuck her tongue out at him. "I knew I was right to call you a beast."

"Come on you two, come into the sitting room by the fire," Mrs Rutland called. "I want to hear all of Peter's news."

The family, now all together, chatted through the day catching up on each other's news. However Peter was very surprised to see that his father was not overjoyed at the news of his Afghanistan posting, and it was not until the evening that things came to a head.

After Hanna the maid had cleared the table, Peter was expecting his father to offer port and a cigar but to his surprise, his mother stood up. "Come along, Tess," she said, "we'll leave these men to talk." She looked at her husband. "We'll be in the sitting room."

Tess gave a quick frown but dutifully followed her mother. If there was a secret that Peter was about to be told, she knew that he would soon share it with her. When the ladies had left, Major Rutland also stood up from his chair.

"Peter," he said, "let's go and sit in my study."

They walked across the hall into the book-lined room that was filled with family mementoes and souvenirs. A large desk stood close to a glass-fronted gun cabinet. The large inglenook fireplace took up most of one wall, and in front of it were two high-backed easy chairs.

Peter could feel uneasiness in his father. Their relationship between them had always been one of friends but now there was tension – and Peter was at a loss to think why.

Chapter 2

"Sit down, Peter. Cigar?" Rutland offered the box to his son who selected one, and sheered off in the end with the cigar-scissors. The two men settled into the deep chairs, lit their cigars and drew on them. Then Major Rutland spoke.

"Peter, I'm now 60 years old, I have a thriving business in the City which I'd like to relinquish in part or in full. I want to spend more time down here on the farm where I want to work on some of the new ideas in agriculture." He paused to examine the glowing end of his cigar. "So I need someone to take over the timber company. Now I know you've only just received your commission but I'd seriously like you to resign it and start a life in commerce. You'll obviously be doing so at some time; I feel that now is a good time as any."

While he was talking the Major did not look at his son once but continued to watch the smoke as it rose from his cigar and was then slowly dragged down towards the fire.

Peter was amazed by the suggestion as it gradually emerged. This was the last subject he expected his father to raise. He knew that in years to come, the business would be his to control but he did not expect this to arise for a long time yet. As a schoolboy he had always dreamed of a commission in the Gunners. He had enjoyed sport and disliked tuition, and had had to work hard to obtain the necessary qualifications to enter the academy. So to give it all up now and also miss out on the Afghanistan posting with the Battery was impossible.

"Father, you've taken me by surprise. I wasn't sure why you wanted this talk, but leaving the Regiment was the farthest from my mind. I'm very appreciative of all you've done for me, and I know that I'd eventually be expected to move into commerce but I assumed not for many years yet. I'll come into the company earlier if you really want, but please not until I return from Afghanistan."

Major Rutland had been staring into the fire as Peter spoke, and he made no move. He again drew on his cigar and blew the smoke towards the fireplace.

"No, I didn't think you would. I wouldn't have. Still it was worth a try." He spoke quietly as though to himself alone. Then he looked at his son who now was frowning. "I've a story that I must tell you. I don't think it will make you change your mind but you must be told of the circumstances that forced me to make that strange request.

"As you know, like my father before me, I served many years with the guns and I was posted to the Khyber on the North West Frontier in 1840." Both men had settled into their chairs – one man to tell the story, the other hanging on his every word.

"I was then sent to do Jalalabad in Afghanistan in '41 with the RHA. Though we were a battery of 9 pounders, we were mainly used as mounted scouts. The officers and NCOs were all supplied with good horses but without a doubt the main enemy was boredom. There was little to do except exercise the men at drill and reconnoitre the desolate countryside. We were at peace with the local nations – but only just. One day in the market place of Jalalabad I found myself talking to a mullah, one of their priests – a religious leader. He spoke good English as a number of the well-travelled mullahs do. He'd been to Mecca and had moved around northern India, and through the tribal areas up to Kashmir. His name was Khaliq. I met him subsequently many times mainly in the market, and often in the company of other mullahs who also spoke some English. We spoke of many subjects; from the art of goat herding to the differences between his religion and mine; or from Queen Victoria to the effectiveness of the rifle bullet. He regularly surprised me in these discussions by the way he spoke of a tolerance and forgiveness. This attitude seemed so out of place coming from a race which will execute the most horrendous tortures on their enemies – and we were enemy regardless of the lack of actual war between us." Rutland wagged his finger to emphasise the point, and continued.

"He always carried a copy of the Koran, which is their holy book, wrapped up in the silken square of white silk with a distinctive Arab mark on it printed in scarlet. He would quote from parts of the suras, (these are similar to the books in our Bible) and amazingly he'd talk of Noah and the Flood, of Lot and the destruction of Sodom, and even of Moses. Apparently Mohammedism and Judaism are of the same roots and have many similarities but it was with his oft-repeated statement of compassion that bewildered me. D'you know, they have 99 names for God, some of them are pretty bloodthirsty; but he would frequently recite, 'Allah the Merciful, the Compassionate, the Forgiver, the Forgiving, the Clement, the Generous, the Affectionate, the Kind.' He told me, and I didn't disbelieve him, that he knew all of the Koran by heart; apparently it wasn't an uncommon ability in their religious circles. My numerous meetings with him helped pass the time, and it gave me a small and interesting insight into their way of life.

"Then one day, in early winter, we heard that Kabul was besieged and old General Elphinstone, with an effective army, was going to retire from the city with the blessing of the Amir. Kabul was only at 60 odd miles away by the main route, which travelled through the Kabul pass, but we had no messages about when or how they were going to leave. We were convinced that they were basically safe; 4000 native troops with 700 British soldiers, plus baggage and equipment were virtually unbeatable when handled properly."

The Major paused in his story and gazed at the fire. Only the crackling of the logs broke the silence.

"Then on January 13th, 1842 at 11.15 a.m. a wounded man, slouched over an exhausted horse, was seen approaching our fort at Jalalabad. An escort rode out to help him in. His name was Dr Brydon, and he proved to be the sole survivor of the whole British contingent. By bad management, weak negotiations and broken Afghan promises, the rest had been annihilated as they tried to make their way towards us through the Kabul pass. The news was staggering.

"Elphinstone, who was an old and very sick man, had agreed to accompany the officers' wives and some of their husbands to 'safe keeping' with the Amir – an extraordinary action of faith in a race that's well known for its duplicity."

Major Rutland stared at the curling cigar smoke, his thoughts back in the past of the Afghan mountains. He shook his head and continued his story. "At Jalalabad our commander was General Sir Robert Sale. A very brave man who'd seen a great deal of action in India and Burma, though now he was 60, overweight and overdue for retirement. His wife and daughter had been captured in Kabul and were prisoners of the Afghans, while his son-in-law had been killed in the retreat. But unfortunately, Sir Robert was no longer a man of action and instant decisions. Our force consisted of 2000 men of whom 700 were British. A week after the news of the massacre arrived, Sir Robert received orders to retreat towards India, a very dangerous action that could have repeated the Kabul disaster. Unable to come to a decision, he acted weakly and called a council of war. Most of us, and I include myself, foolishly suggested that we negotiate with the Afghans and retreat towards India, but in our midst were two men of strong characters – Henry Havelock, a Captain of the 13th Regiment and a Major George Broadfoot, Royal Engineers, who both argued forcefully and emphatically for defending Jalalabad. Sir Robert, thank goodness, was swayed by their arguments. So we set to and repaired our defences prior to the inevitable attacks. George Broadfoot showed amazing enthusiasm, and occasional genius, in rearranging our defensive positions to cover all approaches with as few men as possible.

"The attacks came thick and heavy, with incredible bravery, at all times of the day and night. We managed to beat 'em off with great loss to the enemy and with some damage to ourselves. We even made a number of sorties out of the fort against the Afghans. One especially was highly successful when we managed to capture some 500 sheep from the enemy camp at a time when we were very short of food; even the tough mutton was greatly appreciated. Sir Robert had by now returned to his old resolute self and was a magnificent example, but he'd been driven to action by Havelock and Broadfoot. On 17th April 1842 Sir Robert decided to lead us on a full-scale attack on the enemy outside the gates of Jalalabad. We knew it had to be a surprise attack and it had to be decisive as our supplies of food and ammunition were seriously depleted. It was to be all or nothing."

Again the Major paused and stared at the fire. It was as though he waited for the particles of history to accumulate in his mind before he recommenced his story. "The attack started at dawn. My Battery was split into two sections both with three guns. We were firing case shot, which spread musket balls at 300 and 400 yards range. We'd previously manufactured most of our own case shot with cloth bags filled with old bullets, round pebbles, even broken horseshoes. Eventually we exhausted all our ammunition and the Afghans were well out of range.

"I was mounted on a good horse, and decided to ride round to see how my other section had managed. I rode through the enemy camp that was close by; it was all but deserted, just dead and wounded. Dead horses and mules – torn tents and bedding, all the usual camp paraphernalia. Then I saw a group of four men running off through the fallen tents. I realised that one of them was a Khaliq – the mullah I'd spoken to. He was only 20 yards from me, running off through the debris of the camp when a white package dropped unnoticed from his clothes.

"I rode towards the object and saw exactly what I'd expected. It was the white silk cover of his Koran with the holy book still inside. I dismounted and bent down to pick it up. To my surprise it was extremely heavy. Foolishly I released the reins from my right hand and, rather than carry the parcel away, I slowly unwrapped it on the sand. For some reason I felt the awe of the book but I wasn't in any way prepared for the shocks that were to follow. I gently uncovered the book, pulling each corner of the silk wrap aside as though I had a highly valuable fragile object that might at any moment explode in my face. As I lifted the last corner I saw why the Koran was so heavy. The cover was solid gold encrusted with precious stones. I stared at it for probably only seconds, though it seemed like minutes; then I jammed it into my map case. Behind me I heard my horse give a shrill scream. I jerked up my head round to see Khaliq almost above me with a sword held high it ready to strike."

The Major turned in his chair and raised his arm above his head as though to ward off the blade. "I threw myself to the side as he swung the heavy curved blade. I frantically pulled at my pistol holster flap and half scrambled to my knees, he came again with the sword held double-handed over his head. I managed to pull my pistol out and fired blindly at him. The bullet hit him full in the chest. He staggered, dropped his sword, and then clutching at the large wound, fell full-length on the sand. Still on my knees I crawled over to him as he lay in the dust; his head was turned to one side and I could see that he was dead. One of the other men in the group came running towards me, he was wailing and waving his arms in the air. Unarmed and alone, he dropped to his knees beside the body.

"Then I heard Khaliq say something. His eyes were staring into infinity and his sand-covered lips hardly moved. I couldn't understand what he said as it was in Pushtu or Wazarani."

Major Rutland's voice had dropped to almost a whisper. Peter could hardly hear – but he kept silent, not wishing to break the thread. "Then very clearly, amazingly clearly, Khaliq said in English. 'Rutlandi. When your blood returns here, as it surely will, it will darken the stones of our valley.' I looked closely at him but his eyes were sightless and unfeeling as the wind gently blew sand on to their moist surface and into his mouth. He was dead – but I'd been sure he was dead a few minutes before. I stayed looking at him for a while and then I ran over to my horse. I found the animal had a cut on his neck; presumably Khaliq had caught it with his tulwar just before he attacked me. The pain of the injury must've made the animal squeal and so saved my life.

"I rode round to my other section who were now out of action and preparing to withdraw into the fort. The Afghan army had been very badly hit and was in fact now fleeing back to Kabul. We were relieved a few weeks later by Major General Pollock and his column, and a month later we returned to India and eventually home."

He pulled himself out of his chair and reached out for a log from the pile just inside the inglenook, and laid it in the fireplace. He sat back into his seat and continued.

"I spoke to no one of the Koran, not even to my family when I returned home. I wasn't ashamed of my action then, and still am not; it was fair booty of war, but somehow I was uneasy. I wrapped it carefully and placed it into the vaults of my bank with an explanatory note saying that should I be killed, the package and accompanying notes were to be sent to my father. I discounted and even forgot the mullah's curse for I knew I'd never go back to Afghanistan. But last night when I heard of your posting I realised that my blood will return there in you. Perhaps you can now understand my concern."

At this point he paused and Peter could not refrain from asking. "But surely you don't believe that the curse can inflict any harm on us?"

"As words born of hatred? No they can't hurt anyone, nevertheless the Afghans have very long memories."

The Major cleared his throat and continued his story.

"In 1855 I married your mother. By then I was a Major and aware that the upper echelons of rank were not open to me, so I decided to retire. I wanted to become involved in commerce and I needed capital. I took the Koran and its cover along to my bank manager. I must say to his credit he didn't bat an eyelid when I showed it to him. It was as though he saw such a rare valuable every day of the week. I used the cover as collateral and bought myself into the timber importation company plus a number of the new railway shares. These increased in value quickly so, very soon, I was financially well set up and no longer needed the backing of the jewels. Three years ago I withdrew them from the Bank, unknown even to your mother, they're here in safe keeping."

Peter's heart skipped a beat as he realised the full meaning of his father's last statement. The cover was here – in the house. With a dry mouth he asked, "Can I see it, Father?"

Major Rutland at first sat motionless then he nodded and, easing himself out of the high-backed chair, walked over to the gun cabinet. Using a key from the end of his watch chain, he unlocked the doors. Inside there were three shotguns and two rifles on the back wall. These weapons he carefully removed and leaned them against the bookcase beside him, then he pulled at the centre of the gun rack that swung aside to reveal a safe. The door had a central combination dial; this Rutland now started to turn.

On completing the serial number he opened the door, reached inside and brought out a package encased in soft chamois leather bound with tape. He placed the parcel on the desk alongside the gun case, and unknotted the tape. Peter could feel his heart racing as his father methodically and slowly unwrapped the leather package. A white silk inner wrapper was then revealed; on it a bright scarlet Arabic letter screamed out in its brilliance. The basic shape was that of a number 3 with an extended lower tail but there were other smaller lines also added alongside it. Major Rutland gently pulled the silken wrap away and there, before Peter's staring at eyes, was the bejewelled cover.

"May I open it?" Peter spoke very softly with a feeling of awe. His father simply nodded his assent.

The cover was basically two thick sheets of gold about nine inches by five inches. The front plate and the spine were studded with various coloured jewels in exotic patterns. A finely tooled golden clasp held the cover plates shut. Peter unclipped it and carefully turned the cover back up onto the table. It was surprisingly heavy. A leather-bound book was revealed, inside of which were pages of a soft, almost silk-like, texture that were covered in compact Arabic writing. The delicate strokes were of intense black ink – but as crisp as the day they were made.

"Was it printed?" Peter asked quietly as he slowly turned the pages.

"No, it was all written by hand."

Having reached the end, Peter slowly closed the book and the golden cover, and stood back from the desk. This was not just a piece of valuable jewellery. The book and its cover seemed almost mystic. Major Rutland, without speaking, gently wrapped the Koran in the silken square and placed it back into the leather wrapper. Having tied the tapes he returned it to the safe, slotted in the guns and locked the cupboard doors. He turned up from his task and moved to stand in front of the fire with his head bowed, looking into the flames. Then very quietly, he said, "If I could return it, I'd willingly do so."

The room was silent as both men were alone with their thoughts. Suddenly Peter realised in one leap the full meaning of what his father had just said. The Major was not talking to Peter; he was praying to the God of Islam, offering the return of this Holy Book in order to keep his son from the curse of a dying Mullah. Peter moved towards his father and placed a hand on his shoulder but he could find no words with which to communicate his feeling. The love between the two men flowed through the simple gesture – and both of them knew.

The flickering firelight washed over the two silent men. The Major turned to face his son.

Looking straight into Peter's eyes he said, "Take it with you, my boy. Take it to Afghanistan." He paused and turned his face towards the fire.

"Take it back to where it belongs," he murmured.

Chapter 3

Twice each month, a large P&O mail steamer would leave the Royal Albert Dock in London destined for Bombay. The steamer scheduled for this journey was the *Kaiser-I-Hind* – the *Empress of India*. Displacing just over 4000 tonnes, she was the gem of the P&O in size, quality and speed. Her gigantic bulk dominated Pier 17, and certainly brought awe and amazement to the group of officers and men of 6/8 Battery mountain artillery who, standing on the quayside close to her iron sides, marvelled at her size.

"'Ere, Bomb," said Mabbs. "They say she's so long you c'n get lorst inside of 'er."

"That's good news, Mabbs," replied Bombardier Smith. "But knowing my bleedin' luck they'll find yer again."

Soldiers at the Royal Albert Dock were a common sight and not worth a second look from the stevedores and lighter men, but this group of soldiers was different. They were not wearing the usual dark blue or, blue and scarlet but had instead a dusty mud-coloured uniform. When Major Tenet informed the Battery of its change of dress he also enthused about the change of colour.

"It's called khaki, which I understand is Indian for 'dust coloured'," he explained. "Damned good idea. I've seen too many good men die because they were too easily seen – and killed – because of a scarlet jacket. Damned good idea," he repeated.

Though the Battery was loading their equipment the day before departure, well before most of the other passengers embarked, there was a lot of bubbling activity around the maritime giant. The air was filled with the smell of coal, tar and smoke, as ship's davits and shore cranes loaded crates and barrels of the necessities of travel, plus nets of beef, lamb and pork carcasses. The dockside was filled with carts, pulled by men or horses, unloading, loading, moving or manoeuvring – all avoiding the large piles of equipment belonging to 6/8 Battery. Each section's guns were standing fully assembled, all ready for a single-lift loading by one of the shore cranes. Alongside of each piece was a line of mule harness that was necessary to carry the gun on the march, plus the farrier's equipment and the veterinarian's stores.

Peter and Henry Bulstrode had been billeted together in a cabin measuring 8ft by 8ft with two bunks, one above the other. It was in this area that they had to stow all the 'wanted on voyage' kit as well as to be able to sleep.

Lying stretched out on the bottom bunk Henry mused, "If I didn't know you very well before this trip, by the end we'll be intimate friends or deadly enemies. Hi, be careful, you're treading on my mess jacket."

"So I am, I wondered why the floor felt so soft. Don't hang it up just yet, old fellow, it adds a touch of class to have a fine blue and gold embellished carpet."

"You're looking for a black eye, dear boy. By the way, before we embarked my old man gave me a tip to assist our comfort. When all the passengers are aboard and we're well at sea, on the second day we'll chat up the purser and, by crossing his palm with silver, we ask him for the key of an unused cabin. We can then spread our goods and chattels out in decent order – and have room for our batmen to do their good work."

"What an excellent idea," beamed Peter.

"Yes, the old pater has often used it on any ship where his quarters weren't up to his liking. Apparently the ship's purser is the man who controls almost everything below decks."

Henry closed his eyes and lay with his hands behind his head. "Personally," he said, "I'm going to enjoy this cruise."

Next morning, just three hours before the expected sailing time, all three of the section commanders, Henry, Tim and Peter, leaned over the ship's railing and watched the hubbub of activity on the quayside below them. Some of the ship's officers, smartly-dressed in dark blue with peaked caps, were checking passenger's tickets and credentials, while the teams of lascars wearing blue coats, white trousers and red turbans, moved trunks, cases and portmanteaux to their respective cabins or holds. The whole of the dock area appeared to be hustle and bustle with a large element of confusion. It was obvious that a number of the passengers were officers, military or civil, returning to their duties in the outposts of the Empire; plus wives and families travelling to rejoin the husbands and fathers. There were businessmen going to buy – or to sell, mixing with missionaries who were confidently filled with the Holy Spirit, and preparing to change the world. Dotted in this English throng could be seen a number of coffee-coloured figures – Parsees, Mohammedans and Hindus – all returning to their homelands. Finally there were the obvious and inevitable numbers of globetrotters laden down with the accoutrements of travel.

"Well," mused Tim, "if we manage to chat our way through that lot on this trip we shouldn't find the passage too boring."

Then they heard the First Bell clang out, and up went the cry, "Who's for the shore?" The flow of embarking passengers died to a trickle while the ebb of those who were to remain behind reached its flood. At last the Final Bell, and the ship's siren, told all that departure was imminent. The handkerchief-fluttered goodbye; the last blown kiss; then slowly the iron sides moved from the timber-lined wall of the quay.

As the mighty ship was pulled out to the Thames deep-water channel by her black-smoke puffing tugs, her engines drummed to show her willingness to control her own destiny at the start of her journey. In the Thames estuary a yawl, with the P&O colours at her masthead, tacked out towards the *Empress*. Her mighty engines slackened and stopped; the pilot descended into dinghy and, amid further farewell waves, transferred to the yawl. Now the *Empress* was truly on her own, and setting a course for India.

The passage would take her through the ever-stormy, stomach-revolving Bay of Biscay, into the hopefully quiet Mediterranean, through the Suez Canal and into the blast furnace heat of the Red Sea – finally across the surface of the seemingly endless Arabian Sea to Karachi and then on to Bombay.

Peter was very pleased to discover that he was a good sailor. In the Bay of Biscay, he was not only one of the few passengers who used the smoking lounge but also one of the few who sat in the almost deserted dining room to eat.

Captain Douglas Dainby was also unperturbed by the ship's motion, so while Tim and Henry and the Major were below decks in their misery, Peter and Dainby met and talked. Peter found that Dainby was a man of moods; sometimes good company other times incredibly egotistical or plainly cantankerous.

On one gusty afternoon in the smoking lounge they were talking generally when Dainby said, "Of course your father was in Afghanistan in '42. He was at Jalalabad wasn't he?"

"Yes that's right. How did you know?" Dainby did not answer the question.

"Jalalabad, it was good for him wasn't it?" Dainby gazed out of the deck window at the grey heaving seas.

"I don't know if it was good for him, but he came through it. It sounded pretty tough to me."

"Ah, but it was worth a great deal in the end."

That sounded like a probing comment. Peter stayed quiet. Dainby continued, still gazing at the sea. "Yes. Jalalabad was certainly a cloud with a silver lining for some people."

Peter decided to remain silent.

Resting his chin on his outstretched fingertips Dainby said, "All my career I've been in the wrong place at the wrong time. All the batteries I've been in have now seen action but I've always received a posting elsewhere just before they moved. I've had damned bad luck."

"Not this time though," said Peter. "The Battery is posted abroad and you are with it."

"Yes, my last chance." Dainby gazed at the passing waves now dimpled with rain. "God I must find something in India, there must be something for me out there. There has to be an answer."

"What do you mean an answer?" queried Peter.

"What?" Dainby jerked himself up to answer the question that had been prompted by his mumbled private thoughts. "An answer to this damned Afghan ruler of course, what's his name? Yakub Khan. Confounded upstart."

He sat upright, then jumped up out of his seat, looked at Peter and barked, "Well I've got work to do, unlike some of you idle layabouts." He strode out of the lounge leaving Peter wondering what on earth Douglas Dainby had to do that the others did not.

Tim was completely wrong with the thoughts that he had uttered on their departure; the voyage was boring. Unless you liked the idea of a sea cruise, it all proved to be very tedious. The gunners were put to exercise every day in order to keep them in reasonable physical shape for when they eventually reached dry land. Peter tried to write letters home but the tedium of the journey stunted his inspiration to write. Even conversation seemed to pall between the three young gunner officers; they lazed about reading, or simply watching the sea.

Peter had brought with him two books on India and Afghanistan to read up on the voyage. One was an account of the first Afghan war of 1841 written by General Hawkstone-Smythe. The second was *Travel in the Punjab* by the

Reverend Dampton. This cleric had a very keen eye for the country and the natives that he described in great detail, plus giving information on the flora and fauna – luckily all of this with very little religious interruption. Though Peter found both books rather hard going, he persevered. He eased his chore by reading first a chapter of the military book then a chapter of the travelogue.

One afternoon while sitting reading in a deckchair on the shaded side of the steamer, he was deeply engrossed in the description of an Indian bazaar when he received a sharp blow on the back of his head. He had placed his chair in front of the door of a cabin that he had thought was unused, but the door had opened and struck him behind his left ear.

"I'm the most terribly sorry. I didn't see you there. Are you all right? That was quite a blow."

Peter saw bending over him a man of medium height and build, dapperly dressed in white shirt, cream trousers and a straw hat. He had a well-trimmed moustache cutting across his tanned face.

"Yes I'm alright thanks," said Peter rubbing his head. "It was my own fault sitting in front of the door. I thought this cabin was empty." He bent down to pick up his books that had dropped to the deck.

The man held out his hand. "May I introduce myself, I am Edward Anstruther." Peter rose from his chair and shook Edward's hand.

"Peter Rutland," he replied.

"Of the Royal Artillery obviously, and presumably part of the mountain gun battery on board. Bound for Karachi and Kurram," Edward smiled.

Peter returned the smile. "You're very well informed."

Edward pointed at the books that Peter held under his arm. "Because you're reading those I presume this is your first trip to India. Is that so?"

"Yes. I felt I should at least have some background knowledge before I arrived."

"Good for you. This is the eighth time that I've travelled there, and each time my blood pumps a little faster around these veins. In fact I'm Captain Anstruther and I'm a political officer in the Frontier area. You know, I see so many British officers who come out to this amazing continent expecting it to be totally anglicised. The only concession they will accept is to change from fox-hunting to pig-sticking. They remain within the confines of their regiment, both physically and mentally, not looking beyond the shade of their helmets at the wonder of India around them. Of course some do walk around with eyes and ears alert but alas they're very few. In fact you're the only military person I've ever seen reading about the country before arriving here." He frowned, looked at Peter intently and asked, "Are you a scholar?"

Peter laughed. "If you mean am I a swot? No definitely not."

"Good. I had a horrible feeling that I had misjudged you. Well, Peter, assuming that you have just one inquisitive bone in your body, you will be captivated by this incredible nation. It has all the virtues and all of the vices that you can imagine, plus many more that you never knew existed. I've been involved in the Punjab area for the past four years, having been in places ranging from Bangalore to Delhi." He stopped, and waved to a passing Indian steward. He gave a short order in the steward's native tongue and turned again to Peter.

"This is quite a coincidence actually. You being a rare individual who reads about India before arriving there; you sit outside a cabin that you presume is empty because the curtains are drawn and the door rarely used; while I'm inside that same cabin trying hard to write a book about – India."

He pulled out another deckchair from the rack and sat down beside Peter.

"When I last went back to England I was ill. I had a fever but I was determined to write a book about the India that I know. My illness stopped any writing on the homeward passage, and then friends and relations entertained me so well I didn't find time for writing there. So I decided to commit myself to the masterpiece on this voyage out."

The steward appeared at Edward's elbow with a tray on which were two glasses and a jug of lime juice. He placed the drinks onto a deck table.

Edward poured out the lime juice into two glasses and continued his story. "So far I'm quite pleased with the quantity that I've produced but I'm very suspicious about the quality. I've therefore decided to start having an hour's constitutional to clear my mind before returning to be very self-critical."

"Is this your first book?" Peter asked.

"Yes, and the anguish is such that I suspect it will be my last."

He swiftly downed his drink, and sprang to his feet.

"Well, Peter, you've interrupted my exercise quite long enough. I have greatly enjoyed meeting and talking with you. It is possible – just remotely possible that we might meet again on one of my infrequent outings."

"I hope so," said Peter as Edward turned and strode briskly off to fulfil his exercise period.

Peter met Edward Anstruther regularly as the days went by, and a friendship grew between the two men. Eventually Peter decided that Edward was probably someone who could assist him with the return of the Koran.

Edward was reclining in the shade of an awning on a lounger reading his notes. He looked up as Peter approached. "Hello, Peter. Today I seem to have crossed out more than I wrote yesterday."

Peter smiled and offered him the leather-covered parcel containing the Koran. "I think you might be interested in this," he said.

Edward put his notes down on the deck, took the package and placed it on his lap. He undid the thongs and pulled back the linen cover to reveal the jewelled case. For an instant he froze then quickly opened the book, glanced at one page and with a swift action replaced the linen cover. He stood up, picked up his notes and, still holding the Koran, said, "Come into my cabin."

Peter was most surprised at Edward's reaction to seeing the Koran, and followed him along the deck. Inside his cabin, Edward closed the door and locked it.

"Sit down," he ordered. He placed the Koran on the top of his travelling portmanteau and again unwrapped it. Firstly he carefully examined the cover then scanned through the pages, finally he closed the book and replaced the linen cover.

Peter sat in silence watching Edward's every action. Anstruther turned round and, moving over to the single bed, lay down on it. He placed his hands behind his head, closed his eyes and said. "Tell me the whole story of how you acquired it."

He remained silent and motionless as Peter recounted his father's story.

At the end Edward spoke. "Is that definitely everything? There is nothing more?"

"No," replied Peter. "That's all."

"Does anyone else know of its existence?"

"No."

"Definitely no one on the ship?"

"No."

Edward sat up swinging his legs over the edge of his bed. "Peter this Koran is almost certainly one of the oldest versions existing today. The original Koran was a collection of writings of the Prophet Mohammed. About 650 AD these writings were first bound into one volume; this was copied and re-copied but the oldest surviving Korans are from of the 13th century. To my small knowledge this one may be even earlier. It's of unimaginable importance to the Muslim faith. It's almost the equivalent of the Ark of the Covenant or the tablets Moses brought down from the mountain." He paused, looking down at the floor. Then he said, "Your father wants it to be returned?"

"Yes."

"My God, that's easier said than done. I see his reasoning but this is a terrible two-edged sword."

"But can't it simply be handed back to the Afghan religious authorities?" Peter asked.

"That, I regret, is a naive question made from a position of ignorance. Firstly there is no single religious authority; there are numerous factions that would eagerly accept this relic and use it for their own ends.

"The main fact is that some of the sects would use it as a standard to inspire their warriors into immortality by dying in battle – especially if they had killed an infidel such as a British Soldier. Some of the sects might be persuaded that its return was a sign of goodwill – but for this relic to achieve peace the receiving faction must be strong and true to the faith of Islam. At present Yakub Khan is weak and has no influence over any of the religious sects."

Edward stood up and carefully wrapped the Koran in its leather cover.

"But there is an extra part to all of this. Though this relic can be used for good or bad in Afghanistan, it can also be a shield for you or terrible danger."

"To me?" exclaimed Peter.

Edward turned round, the wrapped bundle still in his hands. "Yes to you," he said. "Your father's name will certainly be remembered in Afghanistan. If you go there you will be in great danger for certainly many of the faithful would kill you to get it back. But as long as you physically possess it you have a shield – without it you would be killed out of hand."

He paused, his eyes looking down at the bundle in his hands. "To be brutally frank, without the Koran you are a dead man – with it, you are in grave danger. Return it to the right hands and some good could ensue – in the wrong hands it could be disastrous."

He thrust the parcel towards Peter. "Hide it well but keep it close to you as much as possible. Tell no one. May be something can be done," he murmured.

The days wore slowly on as the *Empress of India* moved majestically towards the end of her journey. Having endured the agonising, roasting heat of the Red Sea with its claustrophobically high humidity – the open Arabian Sea, with its relatively cooler breezes, came as a great relief. Twenty-two days after leaving London, the coast of India was just visible on the horizon. The occasional fishing boat was also to be seen drifting on the amazingly blue water.

6/8 Battery had been informed that they would be disembarking last, after all the departing passengers were ashore. This meant there were few or no duties for Peter while the ship approached Karachi through the other vessels that were riding at anchor in the roadstead outside the port. He leaned on the rail and watched the approaching activity of the mysterious continent.

"Well there it is – India." Peter turned up and saw Edward Anstruther standing beside him. Since Peter had shown him the Koran their meetings had been fewer. Edward had never mentioned the subject again.

"Soon you'll be able to smell it – sometimes good, other times very bad."

Peter scrutinised the shoreline details as they became clearer. "I feel rather like a new boy at school," he said.

"A sensible attitude. Be aware of everything and trust nothing."

The *Empress of India* was slowly approaching the harbour area that was now only half a mile away. Peter could see the adjoining quaysides were a bristling multitude of masts; many of small and medium-sized fishing boats which were part of a fleet either arriving or departing from the chaotic scene. He was able to examine these sharp-prowed craft as they sailed along only a few yards from the side of the liner.

Edward pointed to one particular craft. "Do you see that large boat with the figurehead of a sword fish? Well that's called a 'hora' while the smaller boats are called 'bheddi'. You can see that the stern on both types is square and the poop overhangs the water behind. I do not advise you to enter into her and examine any of these boats but if you did you would find in that stern overhang there is a detachable box that has no floor. It is the crews' lavatory; they simply sit up on the box and defecate into the sea. Despite this, the locally caught fish are delicious to eat."

Peter laughed in response and pointed to a small boat setting off to sea. "What are those bundles on the deck, and the nets tied to the mast?"

"These boats are out at sea for about ten days on each trip, and the crew always have one cooked meal every day. The bundles on the deck are firewood and somehow they manage to cook on an open fire on the deck without spilling everything or setting of the craft on fire. The nets tied to the mast contain onions that are their staple addition to rice. The whole dock area reeks of fish, onions or curry."

The *Empress* was now nosing away up to the main quay where a multi-coloured human throng jostled with little or no elbowroom.

"Well, Peter, I must leave you. I wish you every success with your journey – and quest." Edward paused and then added, "I offer you a small piece of cautious advice. Try and meet the natives, you'll be surprised how many speak some English. It is from the Indians in the bazaars and horse-lines that you will start to learn some part of the real India. Be careful though; don't venture out alone unless you are certain of your safety. So many officers stay within the confines of their regiments and never truly see India." He pulled out his wallet and took out a card that he handed to Peter. "If you return through Karachi, look for me at this address or at the consulate."

"Thank you, Edward, I'll certainly use your advice. I trust your book is a great success."

They shook hands, and Captain Edward Anstruther left the deck to return to his cabin.

Chapter 4

Fourteen thousand feet up in the Safed Koh mountains, the snows slowly melt in the summer warmth and the ensuing waters join into the birth of the Kurram river. The wide-ranging rivulets eventually meet to form a narrow, fierce, rock-cutting stream that plummets down the mountainsides, gaining strength on its way towards the fertile valley that bears its name. It rushes through narrow rock-sided gorges and past small peasant-tended fields until, in all its glory, the Kurram River becomes a mere tributary of the mighty Indus. There the clear waters mix invisibly with the waters from the mountains of Kashmir, and together they travel southwards until they finally disgorge into the sea at Karachi.

But in the mountainous North, the Kurram has watered many a grateful traveller through incredible daytime temperatures, when the encroaching rock faces reflect the heat in an attempt to totally dehydrate any animal that ventures within their sphere. The hot air rises in almost audible thermals from these sunstroked rocks until long after dark, by which time the warmth is dissipated into the freezing cloudless skies.

In the late afternoon a Pamir eagle, with broad square-ended wings, rode these strong thermal updraughts, ever watchful for prey amongst the tumbled rocks. A stray baby ibex, separated from its surefooted mother, was a prime target; even a colony of kangaroo rats would ease the hunger of this magnificent bird.

He had watched 6/8 Battery making its tortuous way up the river valley that afternoon, and he now saw the domino effect made by the regular camp layout of the battery tents; all underscored by the stripes of the mule lines. The top edge of this regular pattern was furred by the smoke from the cooking fires. He scanned the area for movements but there was little save the cursing, slow-moving sentries, and the occasional duty-bound messenger, while the rest of the inhabitants were resting in the shade of their tents waiting for the cool of evening to descend. The Kurram River wound its way to a mere hundred yards from the encampment, and in one of the shallow pools under the rocky bank the eagle spied what looked like a large fish floating white belly up in the gently circulating water. With a minor adjustment of his wing profile to the up-rushing current, he dropped into a shallow glide that took him down in a wide spiralling flight-path. He cocked his head from side to side studying the slowly approaching object which still seemed to have potential food value, but some 1500 feet away he broke off from his angle of descent and regained the powerful upthrust of the thermal. The man lying in the river was of no use to the Pamir eagle.

Peter lay in a shallow pool, his head resting on a rock at the river edge while his body lay, almost weightless, on a ridge of small round water-worn pebbles. The cold water had enabled him to quickly reduce his body temperature, and to almost forget the aching bones and muscles caused by the unaccustomed long walking. He lay, eyes closed, not sleeping, just feeling this cold environment. He was recalling the last few days of discomfort from the moment when the battery had entrained at Karachi and followed, agonisingly slowly in railway torment, the tortuous path of the River Indus for 600 miles up to Multan. Then, with military precision among native chaos, they had changed trains to follow the Northern Indus for a further 300 miles into the edge of the mountains of Jand. The third change of train was easier and more relaxed as Jand was a very small town where the incoming train was the only one to arrive that day, and the outgoing local train the only one to leave.

This final section of the train journey was 60 odd miles slowly climbing, at an excruciatingly slow pace, into the foothills and finally to Kohat. There, when they left the train, the Battery was issued with mules and their native handlers.

As these memories were dissolved from Peter's memory by the cold water, a shadow swiftly passed over his closed eyelids. He opened them and, shielding the glare with his hand, he saw the beautiful symmetry of the eagle's gliding wings as it regained the thermal. Peter watched the bird rise from a distinct discernible shape until it was a mere spiralling spot. He knew that to take his eyes off it for a second meant he would never find it again in the clear blue sky. Eventually, still visible to him, it flew over the mountain edge to the North on its way to the Hindu Kush. What a wonderful way to travel, thought Peter; to fly, to rise above the mud and dust, rock and mountain, snow and ice. To travel in rarefied air until you saw, way below you, your destination; then to glide down to an ever enlarging world, seeing first the green of forest against the gold of desert, then the shades of approaching hills, and then to see the individual trees just before you land so gently on a—

SPLASH! Peter jumped up as a large rock hit the water beside him. Was it an attack? Where were they? He staggered on the pebbles towards his clothes and his revolver. Then he saw Tim appear from behind a large boulder, a grin on his sweating red face.

"A naked Rutland is hardly the sight to strike terror into the local Afghans, though it is said that it brought fear to the local Surrey girls."

"You ass, Tim," Peter called. "I might have had a heart attack at such a nasty shock."

"Come on, you lazy devil. Have you seen your native muleteers and found out how the mules are coping?" Tim asked. "I have because I'm incredibly efficient, and I'm looking for promotion."

Peter left the water and roughly dried himself on a towel but the heat dried the spare moisture from his body before he was halfway through his task.

Tim sat on a rock and threw pebbles into the water while Peter dressed. Suddenly he jumped up. "This is bloody stupid." He tore off his pith helmet, jacket and trousers. "Peter, you cover for me while I have a soak. I'm like a blasted stewed lobster." Naked, he staggered over the rounded pebbles to the position that Peter had recently occupied then, with an "Oh it's glorious", lay his head on the same rock.

Peter, now fully dressed, smiled and just refrained from hurling a large stone into the pool, deciding to do just that later on. He walked slowly over to the mule lines and to the position where his section's animals were tethered. His examination for obvious signs of wear was long distance in that he stood well clear of the heads as he checked each neck and flank – because he knew that they could bite. When he went behind them, he again kept his distance during his examination, because he knew they could kick.

A native muleteer walked over to Peter and gave a type of hand-waving salute. "Ah Sahib, you have a very fine eye for mules."

Peter was surprised at the clear English, though naturally with an Indian accent. "Why do you say that?" he asked.

"Because, Sahib, you stand away from the heads and away from the heels."

Peter smiled and carried on with his inspection. The muleteer then amazingly ducked under the headline, to which all the beasts where tied, and smacked the neck of a large black mule.

"This, Sahib, is my mule. This is Satan. I've been with him for three years and he loves me like my wife's mother loves me."

The native ran his hand along the broad donkey stripe on the mule's spine, and slapped its rump. "In fact, Sahib, he even looks like my wife's mother, and smells much better."

Peter laughed. "Have you told her that?"

"Oh no, Sahib, she's much fiercer than Satan. He doesn't mind that I say he is like my wife's mother but if he found out how ugly she is he'd kill me for saying such a terrible thing."

Peter laughed again, "What's your name?"

"Driver Assan Bulbar of Her Majesty's Royal Artillery."

Peter raised his eyebrows. Only British mule-handlers are called drivers. Assan obviously thought well of himself.

"Where did you learn to speak English?"

"My father was a driver with the British Army for very many years. He was on the terrible march from Kabul with General Elleefeestun, when all but my father and an English doctor died."

This time Peter just smiled to himself at the gross alteration of the facts. General Elphinstone was in charge of the Kabul Force in 1842 when the only survivor of the enforced march was the Doctor Brydon that Peter's father had seen staggering into Jalalabad. A large number of native muleteers and camp followers also made a safe passage through the Khyber Pass to India.

"My father then worked in Karachi and Peshawar for the British Army. He taught me when I was a little boy how to handle mules. And now I'm jolly good."

"Did he teach you to speak English?"

"Oh no, Sahib, my father made me go to the missionaries to learn the English. The missionaries also taught me Jesus. I am a jolly good Christian fellow also." Surprise showed on Peter's face.

"Oh I am, Sahib," Assan insisted with a twinkle in his eye. "I pray to Allah five times a day but the rest of the time I'm a jolly good Christian fellow. I'm a Friday Muslim and a Sunday Christian."

Peter was even more surprised, "But surely all the other muleteers are Hindu not Mohammedan?"

"Ah yes, Sahib, the muleteers are Hindu," scorned Assan, "But I'm a driver and a Mohammedan."

"I see," said Peter. He did not see at all but it appeared best to agree rather than submit to a long dubious explanation.

"Have you examined the section's mules?" Peter asked as he came to the end of the line.

"Oh yes, Sahib. The natives cannot be trusted so I always do examination at rest times. All our mules are first rate and in tip-top condition." Assan smiled with a white-toothed grin spread across his face. A good man, thought Peter, and one whose enthusiasm was worth cultivating.

It took just over six days for the Battery to march from Kohat to Kurram. For the men who had been weeks with little physical activity on board ship and in a railway carriage, the journey was very demanding. New equipment was worn in, and in some cases the old equipment was worn out even in this short distance.

"Gawd it's 'ot." Sergeant Williams threw himself on the ground and lay with his head just in the shade of an overhanging rock. At the midday break the sun was almost vertically overhead, and any shade was very hard to come by.

"Look at my bleedin' jacket. There's more sweat outside of it than there is in me." With his pith helmet off he was just able to get the shade to cover down to his throat if he pressed his head against the overhanging rock.

Hills stood beside him. "Sit up, Billy," he said in a quiet voice. "It don't do for the men to see you flopped out like that."

"Blimey, Alf, this is the only bit of shade in India today. Give us a break."

"Sit up and put your feet in it then."

Williams laughed, "I don't know why your men don't murder you, straight I don't."

Hills sat down beside the now helmeted Williams. "Cos they luv me that's why, Billy."

"Do you fink we'll 'ave to fight in this 'eat, Alf? I mean it's bloody 'ot."

Hills jumped to his feet. "Officer present." Sergeant Williams scrambled to his feet and stood to attention as Hills saluted Peter.

"The men seem to be coping well, Sergeant."

"Yessir. They're sweating a bit but they'll be orlright."

"Check that their canteens are full after the break. We are leaving the river soon and don't rejoin it until tonight."

"Right, Sir."

"You look nicely roasted, Sergeant Williams."

"Yes, Sir. Done to a turn, as me old muvver used to say." Peter gave his easy smile, and walked on to talk to the resting men.

"I think we've got a good 'un there, Alf."

"Yes he's orlright." Hills watched Peter sit down with the gunners and talk to them. Other officers would have made the whole section stand up, but this young man knew when to push and when to lead. "Yes, we've got a good 'un, Billy."

He took off his helmet and wiped the inside of the brim with his hand, flicking the sweat onto the sandy road. I've dropped my sweat on a few roads for Missus Victoria, he thought. Burma, India, Africa and even Woolwich, and now it's Afghanistan.

He replaced his helmet and stared through the glare at the fast running river.

"She's been good to me 'as the Old Widder at Windsor; seen a lot of the world, fought a few battles and got some promotion. Might even make Battery Sergeant Major in a year or so... Stop that! No daydreamin'. Today is 'ere and now."

He nodded his head; at least we've got a good officer.

The mule line of guns wound ever higher on the narrow road, through the small villages of Hangu, Doaba and Sada with their surrounding fields and orchards. These areas seemed to be surprisingly fertile despite the rocky soil which produced enormous melons and high standing maize. Each village had only the narrow road running through it, and this was quickly lined with the villagers as soon as the battery was seen approaching.

The British gunners, who before entering the Regiment had probably not travelled more than a dozen miles from their birthplace, quickly adapted to the new environment. They were ready to talk, buy or barter with any of the natives. One English halfpenny would purchase a plaited grass plate filled with cooked rice and some suspicious meat in an equally dubious sauce that had a very appetising spicy smell. Despite the warnings from the Surgeon, men still sampled this food and the unboiled water that was offered to them by the natives.

"Can I leave the column, Sarge?" whined Gunner Perkins.

Sergeant Hills looked at his anguished face. "Yes. Be quick about it."

Perkins dashed off from the track and, finding a reasonably covering rock, dropped his trousers and let his griping stomach explode. The sound of his rending intestines mixed with his groans brought forth roars of laughter from his mates.

"Gawd. Must be a storm coming, can yer 'ear the thunder."

"Dunno but I can smell the wind." But Perkins was oblivious; he was alone in his own world of pain.

Bombardier Smith laughed. "It's amazin', Sarge, some of them don't die."

"Smiffy. I think some of them would like to die – just to still their guts."

Finally, at a turn of the dwindling river, the town of Kurram could be seen. It appeared like a knot in the corner of a green chequered handkerchief. The small town of rock-built houses, some of which were two storied, rested on the banks of the river. Stretching away from it were the cultivated fields sectioned off by drystone walls, where the natives grew their maize and wintered their goats and fat-tailed sheep. Spread out in the rest of the grass-covered valley was the Kurram Valley Field Force together with the noise, movement and one eventually appreciated, the smell of an active army camp. A blind man could have described the layout of the camp by the smells alone – of the mules and horses, camels and even elephants, all being used as beasts of burden. He would have smelled the cooking-fires and the cooking of food from the field kitchens plus, if close enough, the odour of the cooks themselves. He would have heard the rattle of the Infantry arms drill with the Martini Henry rifle, the clatter of the dry firing of the new Gatling machine guns, and soon the sledgehammer blows of the mountain gunners striking the 'screw gun'. He would also hear many different tongues; chatter of the native porters in Pushtu or Warziniri, and the martial orders shouted in Cockney, Gaelic, Ghurkhali and even English.

Peter stopped beside the track to scan, through his binoculars, the spreading patch of canvass ahead.

"Looks like organised chaos." Dainby also stopped beside him; his side-whiskers were dull with dust. "I hope they've arranged somewhere half decent for us. Don't hang about now, Rutland." He then strode on with the moving Battery line.

You really are an officious little sod, thought Peter, as he rejoined the line of march.

The Battery was shown to its allotted camp position and at noon Captain Dainby, Lieutenants Bulstrode, Tailby and Rutland, Surgeon James and Veterinarian Surgeon Landsell, all sat on camp chairs inside the Battery Commander's tent. The Major continued reading a sheaf of papers that were in front of him, then he looked up and spoke.

"You're all probably surprised by the size of the contingent here at Kurram, well there is a good reason. As you know before we left England a diplomatic mission under Sir Louis Cavagnari was permitted to enter Kabul and establish a Residency there. This agreement had been reached at the Treaty of Gandamuk, which had been negotiated by Sir Louis himself. A few weeks ago, while we were still on board ship, the Residency was attacked and Sir Louis, all of his staff and a detachment of Guides were murdered. A number of missionaries and their families have been kidnapped or killed."

The seated officers were taut with anticipation. This must mean action – an ambassador murdered; and here they were part of a large force right on the Afghan border – it must mean action.

Major Tenet continued, "The British government in Simla have, wisely in my opinion, decided to take strong retaliatory action. We're going to march to Kabul and return the city to normality. We're now part of the Kabul Field Force and have the honour to be under the direct command of General Sir Frederick Roberts."

He paused for effect, and it was not lost. Eyes were sparkling and blood was racing at the thought of being led into action by such a leader as "Bobs".

"Now for the details. The Field Force will be leaving in two to three days' time. We'll join up with the 92nd, the Gordon Highlanders, at Kuchi, and then proceed directly to Kabul. This'll give us plenty of time to reorganise ourselves into a moving battery ready for action, as opposed to being a baggage caravan like the past few days."

The Major stood up and looked hard at his officers. "Gentlemen, this is action."

Chapter 5

Kuchi – God what a terrible place. A cluster of flat-roofed stone houses mixed with mud huts; all clustered together in the centre of a small valley surrounded by arid rocky desert hills. From a distance the buildings appeared as organised rocks rather than man-made dwellings – but the water was clean and cold which was one, if not the only, blessing.

The Kabul Field Force had settled into the Kuchi valley, arranged its supply route, reorganised its progress of march, and then stood ready to march again while waiting for the arrival of the Gordon Highlanders.

The sooner we are moving the better, thought Peter. The incredible shadeless heat of midday set against the extreme cold of early morning just sharpened the knife of discontent that cut into all of the men and the animals.

Major Tenet had called for a Battery meeting.

"The news is that it's almost certain our march from here to Kabul will be opposed by the enemy in some strength – but we expected that. However the surprise is that the tribesmen are probably well armed. Previously they've had old matchlock guns called jezails, and when I say guns I mean individual weapons not cannons. Well now they certainly have a number of muzzle-loading Enfield rifles and a fair stock of Snider rifles from the last debacle. Though individually their soldiery is poorly trained, as we know it, they're all pretty good shots. So we mustn't underestimate the enemy; they can shoot well and reasonably fast. They also have wheeled cannon; all smoothbore muzzleloaders we think but they've certainly acquired a few Armstrong rifled pieces. Because of this intelligence information, I'm telling you not to unnecessarily expose yourselves or your men to the enemy fire. Is that understood?" A general murmur of acceptance accompanied nodding of heads.

He referred to a sheaf of notes and continued.

"You will all report to the Ordinance Department by Sections to draw your ammunition. Ensure that you take your full issue of carbine ammo. I know most gunners feel that the extra weight of the small arms ammo is unnecessary. Carbines are only used as the last defence, and for that you need plenty of ammunition. The Officer in charge of Artillery Ordinance is a Captain Shafto.

"Now finally I want to impress on you one vital piece of information. You're obviously aware that we are a battery of 2.5 inch 7 pound RML guns, but have you thought how much the Amir would like just one of our 'screw guns'. He could take it to the top of almost any hill and, by moving it about, cause us considerable trouble. Obviously the Royal Artillery never lose their guns but it's more important than ever that we do not lose one of ours. When you're in action you must always keep part of your mind thinking defensively. How do I withdraw from this action? Either positively by advancing or defensively by retiring – if it's the latter then you must retire in time to safeguard the guns. One screw gun lost to the enemy will cost countless British lives. So remember, the guns must never fall into enemy hands.

"That is the news and advice that I've received, both I pass on to you knowing that you'll use the advice well. Finally the orders – we march for Kabul tomorrow!

"We'll march in normal Battery formation with the right section leading as duty section for first emergencies. You'll inform your NCOs tonight and arrange for our initial move off. Our position in the column will be such that we're scheduled for a 10 a.m. start. Any questions?"

"You mentioned the possibility of resistance against our advance, sir. Have you anything more specific about the action?" asked Henry.

"Nothing definite but the cavalry has reported a force of 2000 tribesmen in the area around the Chardeh valley. Now that doesn't sound many but if they defend themselves judiciously with stone sangars they could delay us for some time while we winkle them out. If they decide to attack us in a formal battle, we're obviously the strongest force and so should handle them roughly. Nevertheless, do not consider that this march is going to be a country walk with a shoot at the end, because it isn't. If there are no further questions you may return to your sections."

"'Alt the mules there, Bombardier," Sergeant Hills ordered, and then spoke to Peter. "The ammo' mules are ready now, sir."

"Thank you, Sergeant. I'll report to Captain Shafto." He looked down a line of tarpaulin-covered cases at a group of men. As he walked towards them he heard a voice call out "Hello. It's Rutters isn't it?"

Peter saw a helmeted head appear above the pile of crates. "Shifty! I wondered if Captain Shafto was you."

Captain Shafto, tall with dark hair and moustache, walked out from the ammunition piles holding out his hand. "Nice to see you, Peter – by the way, 'Shifty' is not a nickname I encourage just at present."

"I beg your pardon, Captain," Peter shook the proffered hand. "It's good to see you again. It must be three years ago we last met. Tonbridge '76?"

"No early '77 and we thrashed you by three tries."

"Yes I remember. You were the wing three-quarter and thoroughly deserved the name of Shifty Shafto."

"Ah well, 'Shifty Shafto' on the Rugby field is a compliment I honour but in present circles it doesn't sit too well. Anyway you've come for the ammo for your pop-guns."

"Yes, sir, we've come for our ammunition – and no, Shifty, they aren't pop-guns."

"Point taken," Shafto smiled. "Take your mules down there to the QMS. He'll show you your stocks."

"Thank you, we must get together one evening for a chat." Peter saluted.

"Good idea, Peter. See you soon."

6/8 Battery were disappointed that their 10 a.m. start placed them well back in the order of march. The Royal Horse Artillery were to act as point gunners, which was understandable, as they could come into action in almost the twinkling of an eye.

It was 80 odd miles to Kabul and the Field Force only encountered occasional opposition from clusters of sniping tribesmen, and this only occurred when the rocky hills came closer to be within rifle shot of the column. After two days' march and just twelve miles from the intended destination, at a place called Charasia, the cavalry scouts reported that the enemy were gathered in very large numbers. The tribesmen had occupied a strong position on a long ridge adjacent to, and covering the approach to Kabul. It had to be cleared to allow the Field Force to reach the city.

Major Tenet leaned across the large map spread out on the table in front of the assembled officers.

"Gentlemen, We're about to see action. The Afghans are occupying the ridge here," he pointed at the salient features with his cane. "They're apparently intending to attack us when their reinforcements arrive but General Roberts intends to hit them first. We'll act in support of the Ghurkhas and the 92nd Gordon Highlanders who will lead the main attack from the right. The Sikhs and the 27th are starting a diversionary attack on the left at this present moment. We'll be moving off in about 30 minutes. I know you'll all keep the honour of the Regiment and bring credit to the Battery."

The group of officers saluted the Major and ran back to their sections.

"Sergeant Hills!" called Peter. "Have both gun crews ready for moving off in fifteen minutes."

"Yessir."

Peter went to his horse and removed the essential equipment. Binoculars, notepad, sword – oh that bloody sword. It was an absolute curse when he walked despite having it hung higher than regulations. If ever he was going to trip up in a moment of crisis it would be over that damned sword. Now what else do I need? He stood holding on to the saddle and breathed slowly in and out. Steady the nerves now – act decisively and firmly. What else do I need? Nothing.

"Driver," he called, "Take my horse until I return."

He walked over to the section where Sergeant Hills was slowly walking through the gun crews. Talking quietly, steadying the nervous, reminding the forgetful; a rock of a man. Peter could see Sergeant Williams was also moving through his section checking equipment and men. I'm damned lucky to have two men like that, he thought.

A column of Ghurkhas marched by. Their light brown faces shone eagerly under their green pillbox hats. The occasional flash of white teeth showed as they joked on their keenness to enter the fight. The Martini Henry rifles seemed over-large on these small mountain men. As they strode by Peter noticed their kukri knives slanted across their waist behind them, ready for instant and deadly use.

"Battery will advance." The cry came down the line.

"Left Section will advance. March." Peter called the order to his section. He was walking between but slightly ahead of the two sergeants. Henry was away on his right with Tim further away still. He could see that the Gordon Highlanders, the 92nd, behind and to his left were advancing in column. The enemy-occupied ridge was over to his left, and he could now see the smoke from the guns supporting the feinting movements of the Sikhs and the 27th.

They marched for about half an hour slowly closing on the ridge but moving towards its right. Eventually a halt was called and Major Tenet came back and called for section commanders.

"Mr Tailby will proceed with Captain Dainby in support of the Ghurkhas. Mr Bulstrode and Mr Rutland will come with me to support the left wing of the Highlanders." The infantry regiments were already moving off to their start lines.

"Peter," Major Tenet called out. "You keep position on the left flank of the Highlanders as they advance. They'll tell you of their needs. Understood?"

"Yes, sir," he replied and moved his section to the extreme left flank of the Gordon ranks as they started to move forward.

The Highlanders eventually halted at the foot of the rock-strewn ridge. The first part of the slope was gentle but nearer the top its steepness would mean a hazardous scramble if the defenders were well concealed.

A tall, kilted Highland officer walked over to Peter and addressed him in a soft Scottish accent. "Good afternoon I'm Captain Hamilton. I presume you are our artillery support."

"That's correct, sir. Peter Rutland at your service, Captain."

The young Scot smiled, "I'm Bruce to my friends, and I think that we'll be friends when this day is out." He turned to face the ridge. "Will you kindly destroy those sangars before and while my men are attacking."

Peter could see numerous tribesmen on the ridge but they seemed almost evenly dotted around. He peered over Bruce's shoulder and along his pointed arm to a small cluster of rocks. Obviously a sangar was a prepared defence position of clustered rocks that the Afghans would shelter behind and fire from at the advancing Highlanders.

Peter turned around and called. "Left Section. Action Front." Both sergeants repeated the order and the gun crews threw themselves into the oft-practised drill with speed and efficiency.

"My goodness, no sooner the word than the deed," Bruce's soft voice came to Peter as he scanned the hillside looking for the sangars through his binoculars.

"I'll leave you gunner boys to your work. I'm sure we will be meeting later, and I trust you'll join me in a dram when this day is done."

"I'd be delighted to. Thank you," replied Peter. Captain Hamilton walked back to his men while Peter studied the distance to the targets. He decided to range with common shell at 1000 yards and continue with common shell until he saw what effect it had.

"Number 1 gun ready, sir." And a few seconds later, "Number 2 gun ready, sir."

"Number 1 gun ranging. Common shell. 1000 yards." Peter decided to sight the first shot himself. He called Sergeant Williams over from Number 2 gun and explained the situation to both men. He then told Hills to view along the sights at the target sangar.

"Number 1 gun – Fire."

"Fire!" repeated Hills.

The little gun boomed and bounced back on recoil. The restraining ropes were detached. The piece was run back and the wheel ropes reattached. The gun was swabbed and loaded all easily within the thirty seconds allowed. The shot fell in line but well over the target. "Number 2 gun 900 yards. Fire."

"Fire!" echoed Williams.

This shell fell closer to the target but the small explosion made little effect on the rocks and did not appear to inconvenience the tribesmen who remained spread out across the slope.

"Number 1 gun Shrapnel 900 yards. Fire."

The Shrapnel shell was brought from the ammunition mule and the time fuse altered by the Number 8 according to the scale tables that Sergeant Hills referred to. The setting was put on the fuse and then loaded and rammed home.

"Fire!" shouted Hills.

This time the range was good and the effect quite dramatic. The tribesmen could stand fast against the localised ground explosion of a shell against rock but they were terrified of the bullets and metal thrown through the air from a Shrapnel shell bursting above their heads. Like white ants they fled from the area of the burst and ran towards the nearest sangar which quickly over-filled with men.

"Left Section 5 rounds Shrapnel 900 yards. Independent targets. Fire."

Again the pause of a few seconds, and then the two guns started coughing out their packages of death. Peter walked to the side of Number 2 gun to be clear of the clouds of white smoke that enveloped the whole area after each shot was fired.

"Sergeant Williams, there are two sangars further over to the left. Both are close together. Increase the range to 1000 yards."

A number of Afghans had fled up the hill to be over the ridge and so out of sight and danger; white-clad bodies now dotted the open spaces while the sangars themselves were bulging with occupants. The defended slope was going to need a lot of pounding before the Gordons could take it.

Chapter 6

Peter heard the high notes of a bugle; the Highlanders were moving forwards in line abreast. Officers, swords drawn, were just a few paces in front of their men. A piper could just be seen at the end of a company line. The tribesmen opened a steady fire at the advancing soldiers, and Peter could see the occasional Highlander fall from the advancing line.

With his glasses he scanned the slope ahead to find out where the main firing was coming from so that he could bring his section's guns to bear, for it was obvious that without the screw guns the Highlanders would be in a sticky situation. They were advancing in open formation across ground that gave no cover against an enemy in good defensive positions. But the shrapnel fired over the Gordons' heads was hurting the tribesmen. The flying metal of the bursting shrapnel shells hurt, and forced them to run over the crest of the slope to comparative safety. Those remaining were in the shelter of the rock sangars but they were so worried about showing themselves that they were unable to fire at the advancing Highlanders with any great effect.

Suddenly, with a whirling howl, an incoming shell exploded fifty yards in front of the Section's gun site. Peter had not recognised the sound of the incoming flight because of the noise from his own guns firing.

"Where the hell did that come from?"

He scanned the forward ridge for the Afghan artillery but he could not see any. He searched more over to the left through the tumbled rock and rising crags – then he spotted it. It was a long way off, over a mile away, and it was a field gun! It looked large, and Peter could see the tribesmen serving it. "God. That looks nasty. They almost had us with the first shot – a couple more and they will have our range exactly." As he watched, the enemy gun belched smoke, and eight seconds later another shell exploded in almost the same place fifty yards in front.

"God! What shall I do? If I withdraw, the Highlanders will be without cover. If I stay, that bloody gun will get us for certain."

He looked at the infantry advancing up the hill. They had about three hundred yards to go. "I must stick with them," he thought, "at least till they can charge."

The enemy gun fired again; this time the large shell screamed over their heads and fell close behind the section position, just missing the mules with the spare ammunition. The flying metal from the exploding shell was thrown further on, away from the gunner's position.

"Corporal Hines," Peter yelled at the Corporal in charge of Number 1 Gun's drivers. "Move all the second-line ammunition mules and the spare mules over there, one hundred yards to the right. Only the animals with the ready ammunition are to stay on the position."

"Yessir," Hines acknowledged with a shout, and instantly started bellowing orders to the group of drivers who quickly ran to pull the unwanted mules away from the guns and into a safer position. At least the Afghan shells would not destroy the back-up ammunition or the mules that gave the section the ability to move the guns – and the wounded.

Sergeant Hills moved the trail of his gun to fire at a group of tribesmen scrambling up the slope. He was not waiting for the howl of an Afghan shell that would probably obliterate him – he had a job to do and he was doing it.

Peter looked around. Number 2 gun was well positioned on the left of the gun-site and, when then time was right, would be able to fire at the enemy gun without interfering with Number 1 Gun's line of fire. He called out to Sergeant Williams. "Sergeant, when the Highlanders have reached the bottom sangar…"

Another Afghan shell screamed in and exploded in a cloud of dust and rock; again it fell in almost the same place behind the screw guns. Peter ignored it and continued, "...reached that bottom sangar, train your gun on that field gun."

"Right, sir."

Peter returned to his position watching the Gordons. He was trying not to think about the next shell, for the Afghans had bracketed his position on either side. A simple alteration and the screw gunners would be sitting ducks.

He heard the whine of the incoming projectile, then – Bang! The expected shell slammed amongst the last mules leaving the gun-site but it did not explode at once. It just lay there half buried in the sandy soils for ten seconds or so during which time the remaining animals scampered away. Then the smouldering fuse did its duty and ignited the explosive charge. It slammed red-hot splintered metal and rock spinning around in the spread of a full circle.

A piece of debris hummed through the air just above Peter's head. A terrible scream tore from one of the ready-ammunition mules near to Number 1 Gun. A piece of hot metal had pierced its abdomen, and blood was being sprayed around. The animal was lying on its side, writhing and kicking in its agony, and in danger of struggling into the gun crew of Number 1 Gun. Sergeant Hills lifted a carbine from the stacks, loaded a cartridge from his belt and calmly shot the screaming animal as it lay kicking on the ground.

"Jenkins," he called to his Number 10, "Get the ammunition off this mule, leave the 'arness."

Hills turned back to his position; his crew looked around, they were nervous of the Afghan gun. One more shell a little further in front of them, and they would all be like the mule.

"Don't worry lad," he said, "if you get 'it I'll shoot yer clean just like the mule – but I won't take yer clothes off." A dry laugh came from a sweating gunner; the tension eased as the crew rammed another round down the barrel.

The two guns banged away at the slope. Then, borne on the gentle breeze across the valley, came the blood-chilling war cry of the Gordons. The Highlanders were charging the sangars.

"Cease fire!" Peter yelled the order at the top of his voice. "Number 2 Gun as ordered 2600 yards. Fire. Number 1 Gun move forward to the right, over there." He pointed at a position clear of Number 2. "Quickly now!" Damn, I shouldn't have said that, shows I am nervous. Nervous! I'm bloody scared.

"Number 1 Gun Common shell 2600 yards. Fire."

Bang! Number 2 gun fired; Peter watched with care but the effect of the exploding shrapnel could not be seen.

Sergeant Hills was sighting his gun as his gunners rammed home the shell and cartridge. When all was clear he shouted "Fire" and the gun bucked back.

Peter watching for the fall of shot, saw the Afghan gun fire. Maybe this was the shell that would end it all. It exploded ten yards behind Number 2 gun, the shell splinters whined through the air. Peter ducked involuntarily. As he straightened up he saw that the dead ammunition mule had a companion. Young Gunner Jenkins was lying beside the animal, his left arm flung across its back as though in a morbid embrace, blood was pouring from a wound in his scalp.

Peter tore his eyes away from the blood-spattered scene, and shouted, "Left section, 2 round Shrapnel. Fire."

Number 2 gun was already powder-loaded; Williams set the fuse to the Shrapnel shell, and fired at the new elevation. The small missile arced into the air on its ten-second flight towards its destination.

Peter peered through his field glasses at the distant Afghan gun. "God, They're loading again," he murmured.

The first Shrapnel shell burst in the air a few yards from the tribesmen. Two white-clad figures fell to the ground but the remaining gunners continued their drill.

"Come on. Come on."

Bang. Hills' gun fired, same elevation, same fuse setting. Again Peter scanned the enemy gun site. He could see the last wad being rammed down the barrel; the ramrod was being taken out; they were going to fire!

A white puff and a cloud of dust signalled the Shrapnel burst, this time it was on the ground and just to the side of the gun. Through the dust Peter could see two tribesmen lying on the ground but there was no one preparing to fire.

Bang. Sergeant Williams' gun slammed out another round. With the binoculars pressed to his eyes Peter watched as the next two rounds wiped the area clean.

The screw gunners had won their first duel but only by the skin of their teeth. If at the very beginning the Afghans had fired shrapnel instead of common shell, few of Left section 6/8 Battery would have walked away from the site.

Peter scanned the ridge again; the Highlanders were now clearing the high ground and rolling the Afghan carpet up. He watched as the tribesmen ran along the ridge and disappeared below the skyline on their escape route. It looked as though the battle was over.

The hillside was dotted with white-clad, tumbled bodies; some were perfectly still while others crawled painfully up the slope. Peter could also see a number of Highlanders, some were sitting against rocks while others lay stretched out on the rocky slope; it was their final battleground. The skirmish was over on this hill; time to get moving.

"Cease firing. Limber up." Peter shouted the order. The smoke-grimed men, though weary with the physical and nervous energy expended, dismantled the guns and then loaded up their mules in creditable time. They grinned and joked among themselves, despite the NCO's curses; each one of them pleased with their first battle. They were alive; one mule dead and poor Jennings had a bad headache but that was the luck of the game.

That evening, back at 6/8 Battery position in the Field Force camp, the three officers sat smoking and relaxing over the inevitable glass of whisky. After the nervous and physical strain of the battle, and the fatigue of boiling gallons of water to scrub out the fouled gun barrels plus checking ammunition stocks etc. they all felt in need of a rest.

They talked for some time, reminiscing over the recent fight, then Tim leaned forwards and said in a low tone. "I might be in a bit of trouble actually, chaps."

Peter started, "What about?"

"Well it was damned queer, I was on the extreme right as you know, close up to the escarpment. Both guns banging away, when Douglas Dainby appeared at my shoulder and told me to move my Number 2 gun about 700 yards to the right and into some rocks. He said it was to cover another field of fire. It looked pretty dangerous to me. The crew would've been out of my sight and precious close to a lot of tumbled rock that could've held Afghans. I tried to talk him out of it, and even suggested that I'd go with the gun but he insisted that I send it with just the crew. Well I refused."

"Gosh!" exclaimed Peter, "that sounds very risky."

"That's what I thought. Dainby was furious but strangely not as angry as I would have expected. He just rode off. I'm expecting a call from him or the BC any moment."

"I wish you luck Tim," said Henry. "Old Dainby sounds a bit cracked though."

Peter slapped Tim on the shoulder, "I've got an idea, let's all disappear off to the 92nd lines and find my tame Scottish Captain for that promised drink of his Highland dew."

"Can't, me old son. I'm Battery Duty Officer."

"Come on then, Henry. You and I will go and fraternise with the infantry."

The tents of the 92nd Gordon Highlanders were only 800 yards from the Battery lines. The regiment position was easily confirmed by the kilted uniform of the guards and the men in the lines where Peter asked a Colour Sergeant for the way to the Officer's mess tent. As they approached it they saw a Lieutenant who was of a similar age to themselves.

"Can I help you, gentlemen?" he asked.

"Yes," said Peter. "My name is Peter Rutland and this is Henry Bulstrode, we're looking for a Captain Bruce Hamilton."

The young Highlander stood silently for a moment then solemnly said, "Captain Hamilton was killed in today's action."

Peter was stunned. Right up to that moment he had treated his first battle light-heartedly, with a contented feeling of having won a good rugby match. Now suddenly he felt the first pang of what a battle loss truly was. "Oh God," he mumbled. "I'm so sorry. I only met him this morning."

Henry put his hand on Peter's shoulder. "Come on, let's go back to the Battery."

"Did you want to see the Captain about something special?" asked the Gordon's officer.

"No," replied Peter. "Before the action he offered me a drink when it was all over. I said I'd visit him."

"Then a dram we'll have in his memory. I'm Angus Hamilton of Glen Lyon at your service. If Bruce offered you hospitality then we'll honour it. Come into the mess tent."

Peter felt considerable reluctance at this idea but he was aware of the significance of a toast to the dead man's memory, so Henry and he followed Angus towards the mess tent. Once inside, a mess steward produced three silver-rimmed horn goblets into which were poured generous measures of whisky.

"Now a toast," said Angus, "To the memory of Captain Bruce Hamilton, a brave soldier and a fine man. Slauncha!"

"To the memory of Captain Bruce Hamilton," said Peter and Henry. They both raised their goblets to drink while Angus threw his head back and downed his measure at a gulp.

"Your name is also Hamilton," queried Peter. "Were you related in any way?"

"Aye. He was my elder brother," Angus replied with a steady voice. Peter looked closely at him; outwardly there did not appear to be any emotion but he felt that the young Highlander was only just in control of his feelings.

"Angus, I was artillery support for your brother today." Peter spoke quietly; he placed his goblet of whisky on the table. "And though I only met him for a few moments I was greatly impressed by his character. I came here to strengthen that friendship. I've drunk to his memory and feel that I should now leave. If ever I can be of service to you, please let me know." He put on his helmet, drew himself to attention and formally saluted the young Highlander. He then turned and left the mess tent followed by Henry.

The two men walked away, at first without talking. Eventually Henry said, "It's closer than we think."

"What is?" asked Peter.

"Death," replied Henry.

Chapter 7

Over the last twelve miles to Kabul, the artillery was not called into action again. The main body of Afghans had dispersed after the battle of Charasia. A few small groups remained in the surrounding hills to harass the advancing column with some occasional sniping.

Eventually the large-walled city of Kabul came into sight. The closely massed buildings made an impressive contrast to the surrounding green cultivated fields but from a distance it almost appeared to be a façade. The buildings were real enough but the large outer wall only screened the front of the city – there were sides, and no back. It was obvious to anyone with the slightest military knowledge that Kabul itself could not be defended for any length of time against a determined foe.

The Field Force occupied the main city area, and immediately placed their stamp of authority on it with a firm military presence in the daytime, while a strict curfew was enforced at night. It was quickly obvious to the ordinary British soldier that the Afghan natives had returned to their normal peacetime routine almost immediately. Shops and bazaars quickly reopened and general trade was resumed without showing any ill effects of the recent battle. It was accepted by the British that any Afghan seen in the city was a civilian, and that all the Amir's army were in uniform and out of sight. With no outbreaks of violence, civil disobedience, sniping or murdering of soldiers, it was assumed that the civilian population could be trusted.

6/8 Battery was billeted very close to the Consulate building where Sir Louis Cavagnari and his Guides were killed. The garden wall of the Consulate was being used as shelter for the Battery mule lines to give some protection from the increasingly cold winds.

Peter and Tim took the opportunity to wander around the Consulate buildings themselves. They clambered over the rubble that partially blocked the gateway, and stepped into the courtyard.

"My God – look at the number of bullet holes in that wall." Tim pointed at the pocked marks around the doorway and the windows of the main building. Peter walked slowly round to an old cannon in the centre of the courtyard, still pointed at the main doorway. "Looks as though the Afghans blew the door in with this."

The two men walked together up the steps and through the torn hole of the entrance. Inside they crossed the large hall floor that was partly covered with broken glass and stone, and then they climbed the stairs. At every window in every room, the shards of glass and splinters of stone and wood marked where the defenders had made their desperate and hopeless last stand.

Tim bent down and picked up an object from the dust. "A Boxer cartridge from the old Snider rifle. It'll make a good souvenir."

Peter walked into a smaller room; all the contents were wrecked. "This must have been the dispensary." Broken bottles and medical jars littered the floor; even a smashed microscope tube lay there. A dark stain on the floor by the pitted window frame marked where a man's lifeblood had ebbed away.

As they descended the steps back into the courtyard, Peter looked around and said, "What a terrible place to defend."

"Yes, it's overlooked by everything. God willing Bobs won't put us in the same position."

They re-crossed the rubble-strewn courtyard, passed the old cannon and scrambled their way out of the gateway.

The distinct sound of a distant Mullah chanting his call to the Faithful to prayer could be heard above the general hubbub. A number of citizens stopped at the roadside and knelt on their prayer mats after unfolding them and laying them carefully on the dusty ground.

Peter and Tim stood still to watch what was for them a very unusual happening. A group of devout Muslims were grouped in three rows just a few yards from the two officers. Carefully facing towards Mecca they started their prayers; kneeling, standing and bowing.

"Isn't that your section's mules?" asked Tim, pointing to a string of animals laden with bundles of cut grass approaching the Battery lines. Corporal Hines, who lead the train saw Peter and Tim together and called out. "Lieutenant Rutland, sir. We weren't able to get our full amount of grass." Peter stepped forward and called back, "When you get back report to Sergeant Hills."

"Very good, sir," Hines replied as he walked alongside the moving line.

"My section had difficulty cutting their grass quota as well," said Tim. "I think the QM is going to use native grass-cutters from tomorrow."

"Good news. I don't like my men doing that job. I'd better get back and find out how we make up the shortage." With a final glance over his shoulder at the scarred Consulate he walked with Tim towards the Battery lines.

But the conversation between Corporal Hines and Peter had not gone unnoticed. From the moment the name of 'Rutland' had been called out, the attention of some of the Muslim worshippers wandered from their prayers. Guardedly they watched the young officer and carefully committed to memory the face of Lieutenant Rutland.

As the two officers turned the corner of the Consulate wall and disappeared from view, one of the Faithful rose from his devotions and, keeping his distance, followed.

The first few days of the occupation were spent in organising the Battery and Section positions, not only from a defence point of view but also for the sake of comfort. Tents were still used for the main accommodation, so any spare sheds, outhouses or buildings were commandeered to give improved cover to men and equipment. Ammunition had to be stored with care to protect it from danger of fire, deterioration by weather or loss by theft.

When the Field Force first entered the city, it was rumoured that Yakub Khan's stocks of powder and shot had all been captured at the armoury magazine at Bala Hissar. It had everything – from old Enfield cartridges up to Armstrong breech-loading artillery shells. On General Roberts' orders an inventory of these stocks was made to find if its quality and quantity were of any use to the Field Force.

This arduous task was under the direction of Captain Shafto, Peter's old rugby opponent. One evening, while having a drink at the 6/8 Battery mess tent, he related the appalling difficulties that the systematic examination was producing.

"One thing I love is a good cigar." Shafto blew smoke towards the tent roof. He was seated with Henry, Tim and Peter at a small folding camp table on which stood a bottle of port with glasses, ash tray and a deck of cards. "In fact I like two or three a day but being in that confounded arsenal does limit one's nicotine intake. Do you know I'm not halfway through that damned inventory and I've already listed over 100,000 pounds of gunpowder? Maybe that doesn't sound very impressive but most of it is stored in large earthen pots. A fair number have fallen over and there's loose powder all over the ground."

Tim jumped upright in his chair. "That sounds incredibly dangerous."

"Aha, plus the fact that there are friction tubes and percussion caps all over the place. I've reduced my squad to four men and we all wear sacking over our boots. I must admit it's very scaring."

"Will the powder be of any use?" asked Henry.

"Not for your screw guns but the captured smoothbores will be able to fire it. I only hope that Bobs doesn't want to move the stuff. Most of the rifle rounds have deteriorated to such an extent that they are absolutely lethal – to the user that is, not the recipient." He laughed than raised his glass and said, "Come on let's play some cards."

Next day Major Tenet called the officers together at the Battery Office tent to give his instructions on the availability of the food supplies. "We are buying animal feed from the native farmers but all the men's rations are being bought in from the Kurr—"

Boom! An enormous explosion roared around them followed by more loud detonations. The blast hit the tent and instantly tore the sheeting from the poles as though it was tissue paper.

"It's the arsenal!" shouted Major Tenet. The officers scrambled out of the collapsed tent to be met by the first of the falling debris of brick and wood starting to hit the ground.

"Run for the Consulate walls!" Crouching down they ran towards the mule lines calling any gunners or drivers to follow.

"Get in the outhouses!" Bricks, stone and wood were bouncing around them, smashing some of the men to the ground as they ran for cover.

"Pick him up and lay him by the wall." Dust swirled around the cowering men but the storm of falling debris was slackening. Suddenly a coughing scream came from the mule line.

"Who's that?" called the Tenet.

"I'll find out, sir," shouted Sergeant Hills and he ran towards the gut-curdling sound. Peter followed behind him; the Sergeant's squat shape was just visible through the swirling dust. Closer to the wall, and actually in the mule lines, the air was clearer.

"My Gawd. Look at that!" Hills pointed at a mule lying in its stall. A Snider rifle protruded though the animal's ribcage with the rifle butt sticking in the air.

"Must have been thrown out from the arsenal," said Peter.

"Good job it wasn't one of us."

"Sergeant. Take a roll call and search for any men who are missing."

"Right, sir."

Peter watched him trot away and he looked over the wall to where the Bala Hissar arsenal had stood. A large cloud of dust and smoke columned high into the air, hanging like a large fist above the city.

" Shifty! Oh my God he was in the middle of that."

The rain of dust and rubble had flattened a number of tents, including Peter's. He worked with the rest of the section to clear the wood and bricks from the shredded covers. Some of the tents were torn and damaged beyond repair while others had simply been flattened by the pegs holding the guy ropes being pulled from the ground. Peter's was one that had collapsed in this way and so, after removing the clutter of stones, was easily re-erected.

It was only after he had ensured that the rest of his section were once again properly housed that he returned to his own tent. On entering he noticed that the blankets on his bed, which he had laid out only an hour before, had been disturbed. Cautiously he pulled back the top cover. A folded piece of paper was laying on his pillow. It was the light brown poor grade type used in the Battery Office for messages or orders.

He picked it up and carefully unfolded the sheet. Written on it in deep black ink was a shape like a number '3'. It was the same as the character depicted on the front of his father's jewelled Koran. Under this was written, in block capitals 'BADAL'. He carefully examined all of the paper, and the back, but these were the only marks on it. He sat down on the edge of his bed and realised that he was shaking. He instantly stood up to control his trembling muscles. What was he to do? Nothing? Tell Major Tenet? I'll tell the Major, he thought, because the message was written on paper taken from the Battery Office. It meant that someone with knowledge of the jewelled Koran could easily move about the office. No! First I'll ask Assan, the mule driver, what the word 'Badal' means."

He ducked out of the entrance to his tent and walked back to the garden wall and the mule lines. As he approached he saw that none of the muleteers was there – he looked at his watch and realised that they had probably gone for their meal. He turned to leave when he heard Assan call out to him. "Ah, Lieutenant Sahib, can I talk to you please?"

Peter looked round and saw Assan struggling from behind a large pile of cut grass with a bundle of it in his arms ready to give to his mule, Satan.

"You want to speak to me, Assan?"

"Yes please, Sahib, I think it's very important."

"Very well what is it?"

"Sahib, my honourable father had always told me never to deal in tittle-tattle. He always beat me if I came home with tittle-tattle, though only after I had told him what I had heard."

"You have heard a rumour, Assan? What is it?"

"Oh no, Sahib. I haven't heard a rumour. I've seen something that I think is very dangerous. Two times I've see the Battery Captain Sahib alone in the bazaar. It is very dangerous for him, and I'm thinking that the natives will rob him or even murder him if he isn't very careful."

"Captain Dainby? In the bazaar here in Kabul? Are you absolutely certain?"

"Oh yes, Sahib, on the second time he was wearing a chogra cloak over his uniform but I saw his face and it was certainly the Captain Sahib."

"How extraordinary," murmured Peter.

"I don't want to be tittle-tattling, Sahib but it is very, very dangerous for him there. It would be terrible for the Regiment if the natives killed him there."

Peter smiled at Assan's concern for the good name of the Regiment. "Thank you, Assan. I'll see what I can do to warn him." He took out the paper that he had found on his bed, unfolded it and showed it to the driver. "Do you know what this means?"

Assan physically jumped when he saw the writing. "Oh, Sahib, where did you get this?"

Peter did not reply but asked again. "Do you know what this means?"

"That," said Assan pointing at the word Badal, "means 'Revenge' in Pushtu."

"And this?" Peter pointed at the '3' shape. "What is this?"

The driver frowned. "I do not know Sahib, I think it is something to do with the readings in the Koran. But Sahib you must be very, very careful; if someone has given this paper to you with Badal written on it, they'll have revenge and will die if necessary to kill you."

Peter refolded the paper carefully and placed it into his tunic pocket. He looked sternly into Assan's face. "Assan, you will tell no one of this paper. That is an order. Do you understand? No one!"

"Oh yes, Sahib, may my tongue turn to stone but please be very, very careful." He wrung his hands in torment at the vulnerability of this fine young British officer.

Because of the damage caused by the explosion of the Bala Hissar arsenal, and the increase of information that the Amir's army was regrouping, General Roberts decided that the city of Kabul should be abandoned and the British Force moved to the adjoining fort of the Sherpur.

The Sherpur was in fact more than a fort; it was a large fortified area in the shape of a parallelogram. The Bimaru ridge of hills formed the northern defensive edge, while the other three sides were protected by walls of varying strength, height and condition. Wisely, Roberts had decided to start strengthening this position the moment the Field Force arrived at Kabul. Though the total Sherpur perimeter was over four miles long, with a judicious placing of men and artillery, it should present a formidable face to an attacking enemy. Large amounts of food had been stored; enough to cover a four-month siege, while ammunition and medical supplies were also fully stocked.

Peter was delighted to find that his section, like the rest of 6/8 Battery was now billeted into stone buildings, instead of tents, as the weather in early December was showing that it could have teeth beyond anything that the gunners had previously experienced. The screw guns were kept fully assembled and placed in defensive positions to fire through holes that had been cut in the wall. In Left Section's position, where the wall had earlier been breached, they were simply protected by loose stone blocks erected a few feet in front of the gun site.

Peter had after all not told Major Tenet about the threat made to him on the sheet of paper, and the incident passed from his mind. He was completely safe now as no local natives were allowed into the Sherpur area, and the British officers were certainly not going to venture into Kabul.

Chapter 8

"Mr Rutland?"

Peter clambered back over the low rampart that his gunners were building in front of the section position. "That's right. How can I help you, sir?" A dapper looking, rosy-faced officer with a large black moustache was standing behind Number 2 gun.

"I'm Captain Toby Warburton, Political Officer for the area. Got a spare minute? Want a word." The Captain spoke in short staccato sentences.

"Certainly, sir."

"Good. Let's have a stroll." The two officers fell into step and walked away from the defensive lines back towards the hills of the Bimaru ridge.

"How can I help you, sir?" Peter asked.

"Cut the 'Sir'. Me name's Toby," Warburton said. "Heard from Edward Anstruther you'd met on the ship out from England."

"Yes that's correct. How is he? Has he finished his book yet?"

"Damned if I know." Toby barked out a laugh. "Told me you were a rare bird who'd read books on India on the way out. Most unusual."

"All that reading doesn't seemed to have helped me much. I haven't made any contact with the locals yet."

"Haven't you. That's interesting," mused Toby. "Look here, Peter, Edward has passed on an unusual message to me. One of his agents has heard your name, or one like it, in Afghan circles. Been visiting any of the native quarters here in the city, or before you came to Kabul?"

"No. I went to the Char Chowk bazaar here once only, and that was with Tim Tailby."

"Had Edward's first message about a month ago. Thought he must be on the wrong track but one of my contacts has since heard 'Rutlandi' mentioned, concerning a private jihad. Some one has a very big pot boiling for Rutlandi. Edward's second message said you would explain."

Peter was in a very awkward position. He had not told Major Tenet about the note on his bed or about the jewelled Koran but obviously it was now necessary to tell Captain Warburton. So he related the full story of how the gem-studded cover came into his father's possession, and also the explanation of the word "Badal" by Assan.

Warburton was silent during and after the story, obviously deep in thought.

"This is something very big and important to the Ghazi section of the Afghans. They are intensely religious. The fulfilment of life is to die for Islam, having killed at least one English infidel. Been hearing about a religious figure, doesn't seem to have a name, dedicated to righting a serious wrong done to the Sons of the Prophet. He's waging a personal religious war against us. Attempting to join the various Afghan tribes together. Thank goodness they're so full of tribal and family division, the chance of welding 'em together is unlikely. But this man is their best chance; if he succeeds – God help us."

The two men had by now walked halfway up the slope of the ridge to the rear of the Sherpur. Toby stopped and turned round to look back at the view over the dusty open ground towards Kabul.

"Did your father mention the name of the Mullah he killed?" he asked.

"Yes, I think it was Khaliq – yes I am sure that was the name."

"Hmm, Khaliq," Toby murmured, "doesn't ring a bell. I'll see what I can turn up from my contacts."

"Would it help if we were able to return the jewelled Koran?" asked Peter. "My father has said that he is very willing to return it to the proper people."

"Is he indeed? A generous gesture. I suppose it might quieten the extremists but the Koran's in England while we, have you noticed, are in Kabul." Toby gave a dry laugh. "Here we are in the Sherpur where, in a week or two, we're going to be attacked by overwhelming numbers, and we're talking of buying off these barbarian hordes with some jewelled trinket that's safe and sound in an English country house. Must be mad." He slapped his thigh and with another chuckle started to walk down the slope towards 6/8 Battery position.

"No, the Koran isn't in England. I have it in my tent."

Warburton spun round. "Have you by God?" Then he exclaimed, "Of course, that explains the end of Edward's message. He said 'the eagle's egg could hatch in Azrow.' He wants you to take the Koran to Azrow. "How the hell do we do that?" he murmured.

Peter walked by his side in silence; then Toby looked up. "Yes, that's it. You were in the Horse Artillery weren't you?"

"Yes," answered Peter.

"Good. When the next armed patrol is sent out to the Shutagardan Pass you will go with it. The RHA is damned short of officers. Azrow is very close to the Pass." The two men walked towards the gun site then Toby said, "Peter, you must keep all this information to yourself; a stealthy assassin can get past the sentries."

This warning astounded Peter. "Do you really mean that they have been able to connect me with the jewelled Koran?"

"Seems likely. I'm now in a stronger position. I now know what, or rather who they are after and why. All we have to do is find out who 'they' are – if you see what I mean."

"Where abouts is Captain Anstruther right now?" asked Peter. "Is he in the Sherpur?"

"No, I don't think so," Toby laughed. "On board ship you saw him as an English gentleman with a love of India. You wait till you see him as a native. He's a master of disguise, has an incredible range of languages and dialects, and can mingle with anyone from generals in the mess to untouchables in the bazaar."

Having walked back to the defensive wall, Warburton stopped and faced Peter. "Report to me, and me alone, any contact made with you. Take great care when near any natives. There'll be a large-scale attack on the Sherpur within a few weeks, if any Afghans manage to break in to the camp, there's a good chance that one of 'em is out to kill you."

"You make it sound very melodramatic," smiled Peter.

"If you don't treat it seriously, I'll be attending your funeral. Cheerio." Then with a wave he turned and strode away.

"Goodbye, sir." Peter saluted the disappearing figure – his mind in turmoil.

Next evening after dinner, Henry and Peter were strolling back through the darkness from the Battery Mess. Peter was holding a pack of a folded tarpaulin against his chest with his arms folded in front of it. He had drawn the extra cover from the QM to nail as a wind flap over the billet door.

The two men were deep in conversation as they meandered through the dim lantern-lit night. A sentry acknowledged their presence and Henry returned the salute, then with a flash and a soft whirr a flying knife struck into the folded tarpaulin against Peter's chest.

"Who did tha—?"

"Over there! Stop that man!" A dark cloaked shape slipped from behind a pile of ammunition crates towards the low defence wall.

"By the guns! Stop him!" The crunch of the sentry's boots; a cry "Halt or I fire!"

CRACK!

"Stand to!" A mad scramble of gunners and infantry as the alarm was given "Stand to!"

"He's lying out there, sir, twenty yards or so," called the sentry.

"Bring a lantern over here," Peter ordered. "Right give it to me. Sentry, you cover us."

"Very good, sir." It was Powell. He had dropped the knife thrower in his tracks as he ran towards the city.

"Careful, Peter, he's moving." Henry cocked his revolver as the two men approached the fallen figure.

"It's Musta! One of my muleteers!" said Henry.

"He's been hit in the spine. Stretcher! Over here."

"What the hell was he doing throwing a knife at you for?" Peter did not answer the question.

"Do you speak English, Musta?" There was no reply from the shaking man.

"Yes he does," said Henry.

Peter turned the man onto his back. The blood was welling through the front of his heavy cloak. "Who sent you?" but Musta kept his silence.

Peter pulled open the top of his cloak, the leather jerkin underneath smelt of sweat and oil. He started to undo the fastenings when the muleteer grabbed hold of his wrist. "No," he mumbled, "No."

Peter yanked his wrist away and unfastened the jerkin; there, pinned on the inside, was a piece of white silk with a red long-tailed 3 on it. "Who sent you, Musta? I, Rutlandi, ask you. Who sent you?"

The dying man, with blood dribbling from his mouth, struggled to lift himself up, and with glaring eyes he opened his mouth as he struggled to speak.

Again Peter asked, "Who sent you?" Slowly came the answer, almost like a long sigh.

"Ba-d-al." Then, with energy spent, the life fled from his eyes and he dropped back dead onto the ground.

Peter stood up and spoke to the gunners standing by. "Bring the body into the fort." He watched them pick up the lifeless form, and followed the group back towards the guns.

"What on earth was that all about?" asked Henry in a low voice as they walked back. "What's this 'Rutlandi'? Is there something I should know?"

Peter nodded his head. "Yes there is, Henry. There's a great deal you should know."

On the 23rd December 1879, early in the morning, Musa Khan, Yakub Khan's eldest son, threw his massed army against the Sherpur. The Afghans had an overwhelming force of about 100,000 men but they were attacking a well-defended position held by 2500 British soldiers plus 3800 Ghurkhas and Sikhs. If Musa Khan could find one weak spot or just break the defensive walls in one position, the result would be obvious and overwhelming.

The tribesmen ignored the Bimaru ridge to the North but used the cover of the city houses to belch out in a sudden cloud of men, hitting at various points of the defence to test the response.

Left Section fired a few rounds of Shrapnel to deter the small clusters of men but the Sikhs mainly repulsed the attacks with their fine shooting.

It was just before noon that Peter saw a swarm of enemy troops milling around the fringe houses. He was just about to fire a few shells at them when the whole mass charged out. It was certainly the biggest attack so far and consisted of several hundred men, who obviously felt that the low walls and thin parapets defended by the Sikhs were a soft spot to try and smash their way into the garrison.

"Left Section, Three rounds Canister. 400 yards," Peter shouted.

He would hold the gunners' fire until the effect of the 150 spreading balls from each gun could take most effect. Some of the advancing tribesmen were kneeling and firing at the defenders while others ran forwards and then either lay or knelt to fire. It was not a mad rush but a fast controlled advance with a lot of sting in it. Peter felt confident that his gunners could sweep the area with canister shot in front very successfully; this firepower joined with the Sikh riflemen would be impenetrable.

Bullets were now whining through the air or splintering rocks around the screw guns as the Afghan riflemen closed the range. The gunners knelt as low as they could to protect themselves behind the small front wall.

"Steady lads," growled Sergeant Williams. "Just anuvver minute an we'll give them a dose o—" He grasped his chest, blood pouring from between his clenched fists.

"Sarge?" Bombardier Farrant called out as he saw Williams fall backwards.

"Jim. Give us an 'and." Farrant with the help of his number 10 pulled Williams over towards the high wall.

The roaring tide of tribesmen were now only 400 yards away, and closing steadily.

Now was the time! "Left Section. FIRE!" yelled Peter at the top of his voice.

Bombardier Farrant left Sergeant Williams and ran back to his gun. He quickly sighted to ensure that it was still on aim, and shouted "Fire." The Number 5 gunner pulled the lanyard attached to the friction tube – but the gun remained silent. Misfire!

The canister of Sergeant Hills' gun had torn a hole into the section of the screaming charging tribesmen but they were now only 300 yards away. God what a time for a misfire, thought Peter.

Farrant's Number 5 gunner jumped up, took another friction tube from his belt and fixed the lanyard to it, leaned over the gun wheel and inserted the tube into the vent. Again the Bombardier yelled, "Fire." Again the Number 5 pulled the lanyard and this time the little gun bounced back coughing out its deadly charge. In the choking gun-smoke the gunners moved automatically to their duties of swabbing, loading, ramming and priming. The Sikhs were pouring their tearing rifle fire into the advancing hordes that now seemed to have run out of forward propulsion. Most of the Afghans were lying down; some dead, some wounded but mainly they were shooting back with great care and accuracy at the defenders.

The two screw guns kept slamming out their charges but by now at least four of the gunners had been wounded and two more killed by the incessant musket fire from the tribesmen. The short-handed crews closed up and fed the ever-hungry barrel of their overheated gun, sweating as they cut their loading and firing to almost twenty seconds between shots.

The smoke from the artillery pieces plus the smoke from the Afghan black powder muskets swirled around and obscured the immediate scene. Peter ran up the few steps to the firing platform to find out where the enemy were moving to. But, from his new position, he found to his surprise they were not moving at all. They had stopped and wriggled into cover as best they could to snipe at the defenders. The canister charges being fired by the section were not having much effect as they flew over the heads of the tribesmen. Their positions made them reasonably good targets for the Sikhs but, because of the dust and smoke, these riflemen were having difficulty in deciding who out there was alive and fighting, who was dead and who was shamming.

On the blood-covered firing step next to Peter, two of the Sikhs were lying wounded. He carefully peeped over the embrasure and saw through his binoculars a great number of tribesmen forming up about 400 yards away for a further charge. Things were certainly hotting up.

He opened his mouth to call out fire orders to hit this new threat when a sweeping thump struck the right side of his body. He was thrown in a heap on top of a Sikh shooting from the embrasure beside him. Peter dazedly crawled off of the man and knelt by the wall trying to collect his muddled senses. The Sikh rifleman was staring at him with wide horrified eyes.

"Oh, Sahib, you're hurt very badly!"

Peter looked down and felt his right-hand side; it was sticky with blood, the side of his face was splattered with gore. He felt no pain but where had the blood come from? Then he saw the torn corpse of the rifleman who had been beside him. The remains of this poor man had thudded into him and obviously saved him from the full force of the explosion. He clambered to his feet and staggered down the steps to the section position; the screams of the Afghan war cry getting louder at every heart beat. Gun smoke obscured the area behind the guns but a breeze had cleared the area in front.

From Number 1 gun Bombardier Smith shouted, "Sarn't 'ills 'as been 'it sir. The Afghans 'ave put a gun in them rocks!"

Peter yelled "Canister. Independent targets!" Number 1 gun was being loaded with canister as Smith grabbed the handspike and heaved the trail over. He could see the Afghan gunner working the rammer to pound the shell in; they were almost ready to fire.

Smith jumped back as his Number 5 fitted a friction tube into the vent, and shouted "Fire!" The little gun bounced back on the explosion. "Load," he yelled and ran the few paces clear of the smoke to see what damage had been done.

It was long range for canister but the effect was adequate. Some of the enemy gunners were blown away by the swathe of bullets, while the rest of the crew were badly shaken. Smith saw the Afghan gunner stand clear ready to fire; the field gun belched fire and smoke. He ducked as the shell screamed a few yards above his head.

"That dose of canister upset 'em orlright."

Carefully he laid his gun sights on the field piece, and ordered "Fire." Instantly followed by "Common shell. Load."

Again he ran clear of the smoke and saw that more of the tribesmen had been mown down. The enemy gun was almost unmanned.

Smith saw his Number 2 pull the rammer clear of the muzzle, and again he sighted with care. "Fire." This time he saw the explosive shell strike the right-hand wheel. The explosion tore the gun barrel clear of the carriage and threw it back onto the tumble of rocks behind.

"Canister load," he shouted. "Now let's get the other buggers." He heaved the handspike over to point his gun back at the Ghazi charge.

Bombardier Farrant on Number 2 gun, on hearing Peter's independent targets order, pulled the gun trail over to point at a charge of howling Afghans.

"Bloody hell! They can't 'alf run. Lookit them bleeders go! Fire." Bang. "Load!"

He saw the drivers throw themselves down beside the low wall, and start shooting their carbines at the running figures, but 'them bleeders' were getting closer.

"Fire!" Bang. "Load!" He crouched down low, trying to peer under the smoke when he felt his Number 5 fall on top of him. The gurgling struggling body stilled as the blood gushed from the terrible throat wound torn by a musket slug.

"Number 6, 'ere Nick act as Number 5, Tom's 'ad it."

Gunner Nick Berry pulled a friction tube from his dead mate's equipment and attached the lanyard.

"Fire!" Bang. "Load."

Bombardier Farrant saw Peter kneeling beside his gun and heard the order, "Shrapnel 300 yards. Independent targets."

"'Old that canister! Shrapnel! Fred! Give us a fuse." He deftly wound on the 300 yards setting and handed the prepared shell to Jenks the Number 2 who was ramming.

Bombardier Smith, on Number 1 gun, heard the fire order and acknowledged with a raised arm. He could see the tribesmen clustering in front of the wrecked Afghan field piece. Bloody hell, they're going to charge again.

"'Ere they come!" he yelled.

"Fire!" Bang. "Load. Gawd, how much more can we take? How much more ammo have we got? Just keep going!"

But then they felt the tearing roar as the Ghurkhas' rifle fire poured in and turned the tide. The Afghans were running away – their bravery torn by the incessant firing.

Number 2 gun with only three men serving it, banged out once more.

"Load," called Farrant just as Peter yelled out a pause. "'Old it, lads."

The three men watched through the clearing smoke, the backs of the fleeing enemy.

"Blimey, that was 'ot"

"'Ows the Sarge?" Tiny King leaned on the rammer.

"Dunno. Bad I fink."

Then they heard the fire order of 5 rounds common shell at the houses.

"Come on, lads, one last 'eave and then you can go 'ome. Load."

Slowly the weary gunners completed the fire pattern, slamming the explosive shells into the harbouring houses on the city edge.

As the two guns slammed away, Peter walked over to Sergeant Hills who was now sitting up against the wall looking dazed abut plainly alive. Peter did not talk to him, as he was obviously still only semi-conscious; instead he went over to where Sergeant Williams lay. His condition was obvious; the hole in the centre of his chest torn by a .577 Enfield bullet spoke instantly of his death.

Peter repeated his own phrase in his mind. "This is nothing like Newport."

He walked back to Number 2 gun that had just thrown its fifth shell into the buildings. He viewed the target area through his glasses but could see very little movement. Now was the time to cease fire.

Chapter 9

"How's your Section Sergeant now, Peter?" asked Major Tenet.

"Still badly bruised but he's working again."

"Have you got someone fit to replace Williams?"

"Yes, sir. Bombardier Farrant is a good man. I would like to recommend him for promotion."

"Alright." Tenet made a note on his pad. "How'd you like a trip out with an RHA Battery?"

"Horse Artillery?"

"Yes. Bobs intends to hit the Afghans again before they regroup. He's sent out two columns but he wants to strengthen Brigadier Macpherson's party at the Shutagardan Pass. The battery of 9 pounders has three officers sick; they want subalterns with RHA experience. I've been asked to release you and Henry so that you can be temporarily posted to them."

"Thank you very much, sir."

"Keen to leave the screw guns still?"

"No, sir." Peter laughed. "I wouldn't want a permanent posting but a good ride with the horses is not to be missed."

"Take care, Peter, this is not a ceremonial drill on Woolwich Common. You will be wanted by E/A Battery within the next day or so," continued the Major. "You will only have an hour's notice."

"Very good, sir." Peter saluted. So Toby Warburton had arranged the journey to Azrow at last.

Peter woke with a start from a deep sleep. Lantern light moved snakily across the stonewalls of the room where Henry, Tim and he were billeted. A gunner was leaning over

Henry talking to him urgently. Henry jumped up and, seeing that Peter was awake, called out quietly, "Get up, Peter, we're wanted."

"By whom?"

"By E/A. They move off in an hour's time at dawn."

Throwing back his blankets, Peter pulled on khaki trousers over the underwear and shirt that he had worn in bed to keep the night cold out. Boots and jacket quickly followed. Then it was a matter of choosing what equipment. Revolver? Yes. Sword? Yes, on a horse was the only correct place to wear the damn thing.

He slid the Koran, covered by its wrappings, into a map case that was attached to his waist belt.

"Just personal arms, Peter," said Henry "All equipment will be on the saddlery."

"You lucky devils," said Tim sitting up in bed. "You'll have all the fun and glory while I run the whole of this battery."

"Come on," Henry called out as he walked to the door.

Peter pulled on his heavy greatcoat over his uniform and said, "Goodbye, Tim."

"Cheerio, Peter. Take care. 'Bye Henry," called Tim but Henry was already striding through the lantern-sprinkled darkness towards E/A Battery.

"What's actually happening?" Peter asked when he caught up with Henry.

"We're to be ready to move off with our sub-divisions at daybreak. Presumably we're going to support one of the fighting columns. We'll find out more in a minute."

Henry strode on, then stopped and turned towards a small cluster of figures standing round a lantern. Major Gordon, E/A Battery commander, was at the centre, and he looked up as the two men joined the group.

"Ah the two extras. Good morning. Mr Bulstrode – I want you to command the centre sub-division; Mr Rutland – you'll take the left. My sole subaltern Mr Adam will have the right sub-division. We're under the command of Brigadier Massey and are to join Brigadier Macpherson's column. Colonel Purvis will be riding with us as Commander Royal Artillery for the combined units. Any questions? No? Please join your guns at once, gentlemen, we'll be leaving very shortly. Rutland, BSM Cleland'll show you to your post."

As Peter was being led to his guns he asked the BSM, "Sarn't major, who is the sub-division Sergeant?"

"Sergeant Gritt, sir. A very good man. You can rely on him to control the men." Those few words spoken by the Warrant Officer meant a great deal to Peter.

"Here you are, sir." The BSM halted at the head of a line of horses that were lit by the pale light of the lanterns. "Sergeant Gritt," Cleland called out. "Sub-division officer present." Then he saluted Peter and turned away.

Gritt ran over, stamped to attention and saluted. "Sergeant Gritt, sir."

"Good morning, Sergeant. What is the readiness of men, horses and ammunition?"

"Full number of men, sir, all fit and trained. 'orses in fair condition, though the near wheeler on Number 2 gun is suspect for stamina. All limbers and ammo wagons fully loaded with common shell, shrapnel and case shot."

While Gritt was making his report on the state of the guns, Peter cast his eyes around and saw that a gunner was standing nearby holding a horse with officer's saddlery. The light of dawn was slowly spreading over the area and the indistinct now gradually became obvious.

He walked between the two lines of dismounted men who stood to attention with their horses held alongside the 9 pounder guns. Harness jingled as the horses nodded their heads, their mouths champed at the bits, while dust lightly rose around their impatient feet. The tangy smell of neats-foot oil from the harness lightly tinged the early morning air. Peter could feel the eagerness of man and horse, ready for the off.

"Prepare to mount!" Major Gordon called out the order in a singsong voice.

"Mount!" The gunners swung into their saddles, settled and sat to attention.

With a clatter of hooves, two squadrons of the 9th Lancers rode past the Battery, their horses trotting at a steady pace. When the last Lancer was twenty yards clear of the leading gun, Major Gordon called out the order to march. Lieutenant Adam led the Battery with the right sub-section, and then Henry moved his guns in behind.

"Left sub-division – March," shouted Peter and gently spurred his horse on. The gun carriage horses moved forward with ease. They were fit and the load was light, so the task was simple and the movement fluid. Peter could feel the excitement bubbling inside him at the sheer professionalism and expertise of these wonderful men and animals as they marched out of the West Gate of the Sherpur citadel.

This column of cavalry and guns was a small one, being only 257 lances and six guns but there was complete confidence that they could sting very hard if attacked. At 9 a.m. they reach Nanachi Kotal, a cleft where the road ran into the hills; there they halted and were given a short break. Brigadier Massy called the detachment commanders to the head of the column for a conference, and shortly after Henry, Peter and Lieutenant Adam were summoned to the Battery Command position. Major Gordon described the action that the Brigadier had decided on.

"Now, gentlemen, we've got a little problem. Brigadier Massy has orders to join up with a column under Brigadier Macpherson at the Shutagardan Pass, however he intends to march across country rather than follow the road, as this'll save at least three miles. Colonel Purvis is worried that as the area has not been reconnoitred it may be housing the enemy; the Brigadier thinks this is very unlikely and that the saving in time will outweigh the small risk. Nevertheless you must keep yourselves and your men on the alert. We could well be heading towards trouble, and we must not be taken by surprise."

As Henry and Peter rode back to their posts, Henry said. "This looks like action. I feel it in my bones."

"It's what we're trained for."

Henry leaned across, put his hand on Peter's shoulder and said in solemn tones. "Take care, Peter. Remember, no heroics."

Peter was touched by the almost paternal gesture; he smiled and replied, "I'll remember, Henry, no heroics."

The leading troop of lancers was already on the move, leaving the sandy road and trotting towards the hilly area to the west. E/A Battery followed them; the 9 pounders bumping across the open ground. The advance cavalry had cantered well ahead and could be seen almost a mile clear of the column but then they disappeared around the line of the foothills. It was just beyond these hills that the column would rejoin the road, after the cross-country short cut, and meet up with Macpherson.

Peter was enjoying the ride. The winter sun was now warm and comfortable while the going was firm and reasonably smooth. He dropped back to watch the movement of the near wheeler on Number 2 gun. He could see that it was lathering up more than the other horses but it did not seem to find the steady trot too arduous. As he watched the wheeler's hooves to see that they were tracking reasonably well he heard a call from Sergeant Gritt.

"Messenger coming in from the advance guard, sir."

A lancer had galloped back to the Brigadier and was riding alongside him making a report. The column continued at a steady pace into the line of foothills until it was possible to see a village just on the lower slopes. The advance guard, now moving at a walk, were only 300 yards ahead of the column. Peter watched as a four-man patrol cantered in from reconnoitring ahead. They reported to the Brigadier who instantly sent a message to Major Gordon.

"Blimey, Sarge, all of them orficers look bleedin' excited."

Sergeant Gritt turned slowly to his Bombardier. "And we'll stay bleedin' calm, that's wot."

"Orlright. Just 'ope our orficer ain't an 'ot 'ead."

"That we'll see, Bomber, but I don't think 'e is some 'ow."

After a few minutes discussion with the Brigadier, the Major cantered back to the Battery, stood up in his stirrups and waved the guns forward at the trot. Riding well ahead, he again waved his arm and swung the leading sub-section out to the right of the lancers. When the Battery guns were all in a straight line, Gordon shouted and signalled, "Action left!"

In the dust of skidding hooves, the gunners leapt from their horses and unharnessed guns and limbers. The horse minders took the mounts a few yards to the rear of the position while the guns were swung to face the enemy. But where was the enemy?

Peter dismounted and pulled out his binoculars. The level ground directly in front appeared to be completely clear, then he raised his glasses and focussed them on the lower slopes of the far hills. There, straight ahead of him, was a sight that chilled his blood. Hundreds, possibly thousands, of figures could be seen swarming steadily towards the column. They were being led by a number of mounted figures holding either multicoloured silk banners or large black flags which streamed out behind them. The movement of this carpet of men was unhurried; it was unceasing and seemed steadily all enveloping. A large number of this army were mounted on horses but the vast majority were foot soldiers that were determinedly advancing at a regular pace.

"Battery fire. Shrapnel 3500 yards. Fire." Major Gordon shouted out the fire orders to his sub-division commanders. He had no need to indicate the target, as it was now all too obvious.

Clouds of white smoke obliterated the gunners' visibility as the battery of six guns poured out a steady stream of shells at the rate of twelve rounds every minute. But the barrage was having little if no effect on the advancing hordes. The enemy mass was so large and they were spread out over such a wide area that the exploding missiles only affected two or three warriors in the vicinity of the detonation.

"Cease fire," Major Gordon bellowed. "Mount."

The simplicity of the RHA order to limber up and move, was in stark contrast to the intensive activity of the gunners who in a few seconds had the 9 pounders out of action and attached to their limbers as the horse-teams swept round to hook on.

The Major again signalled the Battery forward at the trot. They rode half a mile over the sandy ground towards the enemy hordes, which grew terrifyingly larger as the Battery approached them. The line of guns swept round to the right and then in a cloud of swirling dust Gordon shouted the order, "Action Left!"

This time the Afghans were so close they could almost be felt.

"Battery fire. Shrapnel. 1700 yards Fire." Peter acknowledged the shouted orders. His scurrying gunners threw themselves around the guns. Then once more the 9 pounders started to cough out their deadly missiles. The lower trajectory of the Shrapnel shells from the new position, meant the burst of metal was thrown forward hitting a greater number of tribesmen, but it was patently obvious that just one battery of six guns was not going to stop this advance.

He looked around the gun position, and saw that behind them was a small village on a gently sloping hill about a mile to their right rear. Assuming that it was not already occupied by the Afghans it could be useful as a defensive position; then he noticed that Lieutenant Adam had brought his guns into action some two hundred yards further away from

Henry's. They were well clear of the other sub-division's gun smoke but rather isolated from the rest of the column.

Amazingly some two or three hundred tribesmen, mounted on horses, were in the act of charging towards the head of the column. The dry ground trembled under the thundering hooves of this mass of horses as they galloped towards the gunners; a large cloud of dust rose behind them.

Major Gordon cantered over from Henry's guns. "Maintain your fire. The Lancers will handle the cavalry," he called out.

Peter acknowledged the order with a raised arm as the Battery continued to fire into the crowd of advancing infantrymen at 1700 yards range. The charging horsemen ignored this gunfire as the shells flew over their heads to bring death to the hordes behind.

In a cloud of dust to Peter's left, the squadron of 14th Bengal Lancers, with their gold and blue turbans, were being drawn up ready to counter-charge the enemy. Lines were dressed. Lances held upright. The squadron commander, with a trumpeter at his side, waited in front of the line of determined lancers until the correct moment came to order the charge.

But suddenly the Afghan cavalry stopped; they had reached a position about 500 yards away – and they had stopped! Then from behind every rider a second man slid to the ground and hiding behind rocks started to shoot while the horsemen turned and madly galloped back to the main body. The British column had been outwitted. Two hundred riflemen had advanced to within shooting distance completely unopposed. These Afghan riflemen quickly proved themselves to be part of the trained soldiery, for they opened a very accurate fire onto the Battery. The gunners and their horses started to fall as the rifle bullets tore into them.

"Steady, lads," Sergeant Gritt called to his crew as the Afghan bullets whined around them. "Remember we make a bigger bang than them."

He screwed a fuse setting onto a shell, and then handed it to his Number 3 who at that moment pitched forward as a heavy Snider bullet smashed into his ribs.

"Number 8 act as Number 3!" yelled Gritt picking up the shell from the dead hands and passing it on to the replacement gunner.

A troop of thirty men from the 9th Lancers was running forwards to lie down and counter the infantry's fire. Their Martini carbines cracked out their bullets but the task of controlling hundreds of well-concealed riflemen was impossible with such a small number of men, armed only with cavalry carbines.

The main body of tribesmen was now much closer; their steady approach would soon bring them to the line of skirmishers. Major Gordon slid his horse to a halt behind Peter and shouted to him through the noise and smoke, "Independent targets. Defensive firing."

"Very good, sir," called Peter and ran over to Sergeant Gritt.

"Shrapnel 500 yards. Keep moving your aim along that line of skirmishers."

Gritt acknowledged, then Peter ran over to Sergeant Arnes on Number 2 gun and repeated his orders. Two of his gunners were lying badly wounded behind the gun while a third was being carried away by the medical orderlies, back to the ammunition wagons.

A scream of pain made Peter spin round. A gunner was lying on the sand, his foot and part of his shin sticking out at right angles to his leg. A wounded horse had lashed out and hit the man with its flying hooves.

"Shoot that horse!" Peter yelled to a Bombardier holding a carbine. "Quickly, before it does more damage." The animal was blasted out of its agony and left to lie there. Harness was also left; there was no time to remove it.

Peter ran over to the Bombardier on the spare ammunition wagon. "Issue six rounds of case shot to each gun." If the tribesmen managed to get within a hundred yards of the guns, it was only case shot that might hold them.

Spare ammunition was moved forward while the wounded were carried back to the wagons. All the time the enemy horde steadily advanced until they passed the skirmishers' line. At 500 yards the Shrapnel shells tore great holes in the front few lines but these were quickly filled by their live brethren. It was now that the keening scream of the Afghan war cry could be heard, and the stoutest of the soldiers felt his guts twinge at the sound of this slow, long howl.

Chapter 10

"Gawd. The Rights've 'ad it."

Sergeant Gritt jerked his head towards Lieutenant Adam's right sub-division. A swarm of Afghans had poured out of a dried-up nullah only fifty yards in front of the two guns; the horse gunners were being cut down before they could draw their carbines to fight. Behind, Peter heard the thunder of hooves and the shouts of commands as the squadron of the 14th Bengal Lancers charged across to tear into the melee around the guns. In that short distance the pennants fluttered, lances dipped and their tips turned red as the riders picked their target.

The lancers slammed into the seething mass of tribesmen but the enemy numbers were far too great and the sheer mass stopped the cavalry from riding through. Lances were dropped and sabres drawn. Up and down went the curved blades until the position was almost cleared when yet a further mass of Afghans appeared from the nearby nullah.

Above the screams and shouts came the urgent notes as the 14th Bengal trumpeter sounded 'Recall'. Desperately fighting, the remaining lancers slowly began to withdraw. Eventually clear they prepared to charge again in an attempt to stem this unexpected surge – but the 9 pounders were being abandoned.

Major Gordon galloped up to Peter; he leaned down and shouted. "Be prepared to withdraw to that village behind us. Sweep round to the right, there's a large ditch directly in front. Position yourself behind the wall." He pointed at a low wall leading from the mud houses, "The Lancers'll charge the enemy just as you retire. We've heard that Brigadier

Macpherson is sending guns and infantry to assist but we must hold on for another hour or so."

"Very good, sir. Any news of Mr Adam?" Gordon shook his head and pulled his horse around to gallop over to Henry.

Peter shouted to the ammunition teams. "Ride for the village. Get the wagons ready. Keep the horses protected in the trees if you can. Now GO!"

He could see the 9th Lancers already forming up to charge the head of the enemy but noticed that the flanks of the Afghans were even now overlapping the guns and the Lancers. If the Afghans advanced another hundred yards they would be able to fire onto the column's positions from the undefended side.

He ran over to Sergeant Gritt and shouted to him through the tearing gunfire, "We're moving back to the village soon. Mind the ditch in front of it. Keep well over to the right."

Gritt nodded and twisted the fuse on yet another shell. As Peter turned towards Sergeant Arnes he heard the lancer's trumpeter sound the charge.

"Cease fire! Mount!" screamed Peter at his Number 2 gun.

Sergeant Arnes, a bloody bandage around the wound in his head, acknowledged and waved his arms frantically for his limber horses, then single-handed he lifted up the gun trail. In a dust-showering arc the six-horse team swept round under the control of only two gunners. The limber stopped within six feet of the gun trail. Peter threw himself against the gun's right wheel and, with Arnes struggling to hold the trail up on his own, they slowly bumped the gun over the rocky ground to latch onto the limber hook. Glancing to his right he saw Sergeant Gritt's team already cantering towards the village. BSM Cleland was helping a wounded gunner onto Number 2 limber; there were other gunners strewn on the rocky soil but they were lying completely still. Dead men could not be allowed to hinder the living.

A loose horse trotted by; Peter caught it and jumped into the saddle then waved the gun team on towards the village; suddenly he remembered the Major's warning about the ditch. He kicked his horse on and galloped up to the team leader, frantically waving at him to move further over to the right.

"Swing over to the right," Peter yelled. "There's a ditch ahead."

The gun and limber bounced behind the galloping team with two gunners desperately holding on to a wounded mate; he was probably dead already.

Peter saw the ditch end just a few yards away on his left. It ran in front of the village and was about six foot deep. It was too wide for a horse to jump and just too narrow to ride into and out of. He spurred his horse on and, in a mad gallop, led Number 2 gun team towards the orchard where Sergeant Gritt was already coming into action.

All the survivors of the Bengal Lancers were lying down behind rocks in front of the village waiting for the enemy to come within range of their carbines. Through the swirling dust Peter could see the second squadron of the 9th Lancers smash into the enemy head trying to extricate their first squadron. But they were dying to a man. Henry's guns were now only twenty yards clear of the leading tribesmen, and his gunners were frantically pulling their pieces round to limber up.

"Sergeant Gritt. Fire Shrapnel to support the Centres. Sergeant Arnes, Shrapnel to support the Lancers." It was all hopelessly inadequate but it might just help. He ran back to the ammunition wagons. The horse teams could be halter-tied to the scrubby olive trees in the orchard, and the spare men used to carry ammunition and man the guns.

"Hitch your teams up and get to the guns. NOW!" he yelled at the ammunition wagon drivers. The limber teams must remain manned in case a further withdrawal was necessary – though where to retreat to, God only knew.

Peter saw BSM Cleland acting as a Number 3 on Sergeant Gritt's gun, and sent a horse holder over to replace him. "Sarn't major, we'll move the remaining ammunition from the wagons to the ready limber."

"Here come the Centres!"

Peter looked up and saw the two teams galloping out of action straight towards the village. "Oh God. Henry doesn't know about the ditch," Peter cried.

He sprinted out of the orchard and, vaulting over the low wall, ran towards the ditch waving his arms and yelling to the teams to swing away to their right but the riders ignored his gesticulations right up to the time that the lead horses disappeared down into the ditch. Amazingly they both came out the other side, so did the next pair – but, in a cloud of dust, the wheelers fell. The riding gunners jumped from their saddles and started tugging vainly at the bridles to help their mounts get that extra pulling power but it was obviously useless.

"Cut the traces," yelled Peter.

A Sergeant, blood pouring from a wound in his neck, slashed at the leather traces with his sword and the four front horses leapt free.

Henry cantered up with his other gun and calmly viewed the dismal scene of his wrecked piece.

"Henry, the ditch end is two hundred yards up there," Peter called pointing to his left. Henry looked behind him at the swarm of tribesmen now only a couple of hundred yards away. He could see that his flank was sealed; the lancers had pulled back beyond the ditch end.

"Peter, take my men and horses back. I'll spike the guns."

It was the only thing to do; it was disastrous but it was inevitable. The centre sub-division gunners freed their horses and pulled them by their heads down into the ditch and scampered out the other side. They ran into the orchard, and threw themselves onto the guns of Sergeant Gritt and Arnes.

"Henry, give me a spike for the gun in the ditch."

"They're my guns, Peter."

"No heroics, Henry!"

"They are my guns."

There was no point in arguing. Peter turned and, bending low, ran back to his sub-division. He glimpsed through the white gun smoke, a figure trotting purposefully towards the ditch. It was BSM Cleland.

"Sarn't Major," yelled Peter, "Mr Bulstrode wants to spike the guns himself."

"He'll need some help then, sir," Cleland replied calmly as he continued towards the ditch at a steady trot.

The scream of Shrapnel shells flying overhead made Peter wince as he ran back to his guns. Both pieces were now fully manned and the ready ammunition was well stacked. The Lancers were putting up a hot fire from their protected position and it looked as though the Afghans were being held or at least slowed down as, at point blank range, the bullets and shells tore into them.

Peter knelt by the wall and saw Henry clamber out of the ditch having spiked the wrecked gun, then run towards the other gun on the far side but the charging tribesmen were almost on it. BSM Cleland clambered out of the ditch and followed Henry, pulling out his sword as he ran.

"Sergeant Gritt! Give covering fire to the centre gun."

It was almost impossible to fire close enough to help but not so close as to wound friends. Henry reached the gun and pulled out a spiking-nail; a screaming tribesman threw a spear over the 9 pounder's barrel and hit him fully in the chest but though Henry staggered he seemed to ignore the wound as he struck at the spiking nail with his hammer. BSM Cleland slashed at a warrior coming round the left wheel and felled him. Henry struck with the hammer again and again and again.

"Come on, Henry, that'll do," cried Peter to himself in anguish. "No heroics."

But the moment Henry felt that the spike was fully and firmly home he knew his job was completed; slowly he slumped down onto his knees by the axle. Cleland kept slashing and parrying with his sword until the gun and its two brave men disappeared under the swamping surf of the howling horde. The charging tribesmen paused at the edge of the ditch only one hundred yards away; they hesitated in the face of the intense carbine fusillade from the lancers and the two 9 pounders. "Reverse Shrapnel!" Peter yelled. The Shrapnel shell was to be inserted into the barrel, unfused and nose first. On firing the shell would burst and be thrown out like case shot hundreds of pieces of flying metal.

"Sergeant Gritt, lay on the centre gun."

Gritt did not reply; he just did his duty. He knew that the shell would kill everyone on the gun including the officer and the BSM, if they were still alive. But better they should be dead than suffer an agonising death in the hands of the Afghans.

Gritt's gun barked out its tearing death. Peter watched as the shell tore red strips into the maddened warriors; he watched as gun wheels were smashed; he watched as he pronounced Lieutenant H. Bulstrode and Battery Sergeant Major Cleland – officially dead!

Lancers and gunners sweated as rifle barrels grew too hot to hold and gun barrels seared the hand that touched them while they slammed away at the solid enemy wall.

"Keep firing, Lieutenant," Major Gordon called out. Peter turned and saw the Battery Commander walking towards him. He had no helmet; his right arm was hanging by his side with blood dripping off his fingers.

"Hold on, gunners!" he shouted, "The Ghurkhas are on their way." Gordon looked ready to fall, his face was ashen.

"We must hold on a little longer. A mountain battery and the 4th Ghurkhas will be attacking the enemy flank very soon. When they do, and the effect starts to show, the Brigadier'll send in the 9th Lancers – or what's left of them."

Surely it was not possible. How could they hold out? To the left the enemy had already overlapped the defences in the area behind the ditches. All the Afghans had to do was to move more men into that quarter and the lancers would be swamped.

"That's the last of the ammunition from the spare wagons sir." A Sergeant from Henry's guns stood in front of Peter. His right arm was tied in a sling across his chest; a crude bandage covered the stump where his hand had been while the grey, dirt-covered face told of the pain that the man was suffering. Peter ran over to the piles of ready ammunition behind the guns. They were horrifyingly small, just a cluster of shells.

"Sergeant Gritt. Select your targets carefully, that's all the ammunition you have."

Gritt, with powder-blackened face and red-rimmed eyes, smiled and re-aligned the gun again. He could fire it with his eyes closed and still hit the enemy. "Very good, sir, I'll be careful."

Peter caught the ironic tone of Gritt's reply; he smiled in return and slapped the Sergeant on his back then ran back to the group of wounded men by the spare wagons.

"If any of you can walk or fire a carbine, get hold of one now. Very soon we're going to need every bit of help."

The wounded Sergeant staggered over, handing out the spare carbines and bandoliers of ammunition. Some of the gunners could only sit up if they were leant against a tree or a wheel but they were determined to die fighting; they would save the last round to blow their own brains out.

Peter looked over his guns towards the enemy. There seemed to be a general movement of the hostile force towards the right flank. Presumably they intended to break through by way of the village. The Afghans must assume there was plentiful ammunition for the 9 pounders to cover the open ground, and if they could attack from the mud houses they would be protected from the gunfire. Unknown to the Afghans, the guns would be starved of shells and would be standing there silent. The movement of the tribesmen seemed to be growing, even some of the men firing from the ditch were now moving away towards the right.

The scream of an incoming shell howled through the air; a missile exploded 200 yards in front of the village wall in a cloud of dust.

"Oh God. The Afghans've brought in a field gun to silence us!"

Then more shells started falling further away from the village and exploding into the enemy lines. The steeply angled trajectory even had the occasional projectile falling directly into the ditch itself with startling effect. Peter grabbed his binoculars and scrutinised the left front where the mountain battery and the Ghurkhas were to come from but the area was empty. More shells crashed into the enemy ranks precipitating a faster movement of Afghans towards the right flank.

"It's Macpherson's field artillery," croaked Major Gordon "Look. Beyond the tribesmen. They must've come off the road."

The enemy were now steadily flowing away to the right of the village in large numbers. Obviously that was their escape route; to turn to the left would mean facing the Ghurkhas who could not be far away. A steady succession of shells from the field artillery now dotted the rapidly thinning ranks of the Afghans until eventually only the wounded and dead remained. The air was filled with the moans and screams of wounded and dying, of both sides.

"E/A Battery cease fire!" called Major Gordon.

As the powder smoke and dust drifted sway, the defenders could see a steadily approaching line of the relief troops. Peter looked at the two 9 pounders guns and the weary horse gunners. The men were all too tired to cheer; they stood like dead men, exhaustion written on every powder-blackened face. Sergeant Arnes replaced the shell, that he was about to use, back with the ready ammunition; there were only seven rounds left on the pile behind his gun, while behind Number 1 gun only two shells remained.

"I never want to be in anything as close as that ever again." Major Gordon spoke quietly, possibly to himself but also on behalf of every grateful man left alive in that blood soaked orchard.

Some hours later the remnants of the 9th and 18th Lancers plus the survivors of E/A Battery rode out from the bullet-pocked mud village to join up with Brigadier Macpherson's force, at the little town of Killa Khazi. The Brigadier had sent out cavalry patrols to ride over the battlefield and bring in the dead and the lucky few wounded who had survived and not been captured.

Henry's body and that of BSM Cleland were recovered from the wheels of his gun. They were sent with the other dead, under escort, back to Kabul to be buried with full military honours at the military cemetery at the Sherpur.

But the recent dead were among the fortunate ones for throughout that night the Afghan women started torturing the British wounded that their menfolk had removed from the battlefield. The tribeswomen returned to within half a mile of the encamped force carrying the wounded men with them and then, within the protective confines of a dried-up nullah or pit, started to slowly disembowel or flay the poor wretches. Their demented screams tore through the night and into the British lines as their souls were slowly dragged from their tortured bodies by skilful blood-soaked hands. Four times during the night the column's guns fired star shells followed by a pattern of Shrapnel trying to stop the fiendish acts and hopefully to end the excruciating torment of their suffering victims.

Next morning cavalry patrols were again sent out. This time they brought in a number of tarpaulin-wrapped bundles of lacerated cadavers barely recognisable as ever having been human beings. The troopers, who returned from this nauseous task, were soul-scarred in their hatred that could inflict such fiendish atrocities on defenceless men.

The survivors of E/A battery rode back to Kabul. The four guns lost in battle were recovered from the field so the battery returned with all its six guns in tow.

Henry's death weighed heavily on Peter's mind. As though to perpetually remind him, he continuously felt the dead weight of the jewelled Koran in the map-case hanging from his belt. It had been with him throughout the battle and now once more it was returning to Kabul.

Will I never be rid of it – and that damned curse? he thought – but he could find no answer.

Chapter 11

As the full spate of bitter winter descended onto the Field Force encamped at the Sherpur, it became obvious to all of the men that the Afghan army was defeated, demoralised and even destroyed.

Macpherson's and Baker's columns had attacked and dispersed those tribesmen who were gathering after the terrible defeat Musa Khan's army suffered in the Sherpur attack. It was obvious that the Afghans would not attack again. In the Kandahar area, the local Governor or Wali had even raised levies of militia to assist the British keep peace, and prove his acceptance of their rule.

Political and diplomatic moves were made to the Amir, Yakub Khan, who showed acceptance of the situation and complied with the conditions laid down by the British government. These were to accept a British Embassy, refuse a Russian one and to pay financial compensation for the trouble caused during the recent unpleasantness. The North West approaches to India were safe.

The men in the Sherpur garrison were confident of an early move back to India and then possibly "dear old Blighty". Peter and Tim were hoping for a posting to India, for a year or so, after a few months' leave. Though the Afghans remained peaceful there was little contact by the soldiers with the natives in Kabul. Stores were bought for the garrison from the local wily traders who made extortionate profits from the British commissariat. No British officer was allowed into the city unless on business, and strictly no natives were allowed into the Sherpur.

Then in late July came the news that no one wanted to hear; Ayub Khan, a younger brother of Yakub Khan, had succeeded in uniting the border tribes in south-western Afghanistan. The British area commander in Kandahar, Major General Primrose had sent out a force of two regiments of Indian cavalry, three infantry battalions and an RHA battery of 9 pounders to control the insurgents.

But at Maiwand, the British force was defeated and thrown back to Kandahar where they were now besieged by the victorious Ayub Khan.

"Harrumph," coughed Major Tenet, always the start of momentous news. All the battery officers were seated in front of him.

"Well, gentlemen, as you're aware, the British force at Kandahar has suffered a reverse – a reverse of some magnitude – not to put too fine a point on it – a damned disaster!" he paused, both of his clenched fists placed firmly on the table in front of him on which rested a sheaf of papers.

"General Roberts has decided that the city of Kandahar must be relieved and then…" Tenet raised his voice and his gaze to cover the assembled officers, "then the army of Ayub Khan must be totally defeated."

No one stirred, they all either knew or guessed these facts. The questions they wanted answered were: When, how and by whom?

"The general will be taking a Relief Force of 10,000 to Kandahar. These will join with the city defenders to defeat, once and for all, the Afghan army. Now there is a surprise in the decision of the formation of this relief column. He's not taking any wheeled artillery."

Now that was news!

"General Roberts has decided that as the road there can be poor to non-existent, and because he wants a speedy journey, he'll only take cavalry, infantry and the mountain gunners." He turned from the papers on his desk and again looked at his officers.

"In fact this venture of the General's has some very worrying aspects. Though we'll be a very strong force and able to move with creditable speed, we'll be without a base to fall back on, or any means of support. Plus, having arrived at Kandahar, we have to raise a siege against an enemy that's vastly superior in strength. We'll be on our own, win or lose. The sooner we start, the less chance Ayub Khan'll have of summoning up an attack on us en route. Now for the details." Tenet selected a sheet of paper that he referred to as he further addressed his officers.

"We'll be with the 1st Infantry Brigade, attached to which will be Section A Field Hospital. The Commander Royal Artillery for the force will be Colonel Johnson. We'll retain our normal mule contingent at full strength but each officer will only be allotted one animal for his kit. Our artillery reserve will carry 30 rounds per gun." He looked up and added, "We'll be leaving at first light tomorrow. Any questions?"

"How will the sick be carried, sir? Presumably there'll be no wheeled ambulances," asked Tim.

"You're quite correct," replied the Major, and again he referred to his notes. "Sick and wounded'll be carried on dhoolies and dandies; native bearers will be supplied."

"What exactly are dhoolies and dandies, sir?"

"Aha, a dhoolie is a litter slung from a camel or horse, while a dandy is a hammock attached to a pole and carried by two natives."

"Good Lord. Thank you, sir."

"Now any more questions? Then, gentlemen, return to your sections and prepare for our movement tomorrow at dawn."

With typical efficiency the column started at daybreak and all three Brigades wound their way across the country on the start of their journey of more than 300 miles to Kandahar across mountain and river, cultivated field and desert.

The headmen of the Warduks, Hazaras and Ghilzias, whose country the column would pass through, were instructed to collect and prepare necessary supplies to feed and water the men and animals. Animal fodder was normally easy to obtain because of the standing green-crops in the fertile valleys along the side parts of the road. The owners eagerly sold these crops to the British Quartermasters who paid well for them in Indian Rupees.

The daily start became earlier and earlier because of the incredible heat experienced by midday. The column always halted between 1 and 2 p.m. to encamp when the thermometer frequently reached 95 degrees in the shade − except there was no shade. The journey was gruelling to man and beast as they all suffered from heat and lack of water by day, then cold and sometimes further lack of water by night.

On the rolling countryside the tribesmen were friendly, or at least showed friendliness. There was no true opportunity to attack or ambush the column but further on, when the hills encroached onto the road, opportunities for attacking would benefit any well-hidden tribesmen.

Peter and Tim often walked their horses. They had decided to use their mounts only when it was really necessary and also to march rather than ride because the men were marching.

Striding through the rising dust, Tim touched Peter's arm and spoke quietly to him. "Have you seen the BC recently? I think he's very ill; he's beginning to look quite grey to me."

"Now you've mentioned it he has been rather quiet of late."

"God just imagine," mused Tim. "If he went down sick, we'd have Dainby as BC. Heaven help us then."

Peter laughed. "You've got a down on Dainby. He is strange I admit, but he's a good gunner."

"Is he? I still remember that nonsense I had with him before Kabul."

After two weeks of relentless marching the Kandahar Relief Force reached Baba Kazai where they rested for 24 hours. They had travelled over 200 miles, averaging 15 miles each day. This was an amazing rate of progress when the incredibly high daytime temperatures and the lack of water were taken into account. Bobs was determined to travel fast but also to ensure that his men in his column were all fit to fight when he arrived at Kandahar. He drove them hard – but not too hard.

The next day they had only marched three miles after the midday break, when the column stopped. They waited for a couple of hours; then the order came for the Battery to make camp for the night within their own position of march.

"Good God!" exclaimed Tim, "We'll be dining damned near the mules tonight. Have you any idea why our sleeping arrangements are being so greatly inconvenienced? Much more of this and I'll have to start staying at my club. All very annoying. What?"

"And with no hot water for your bath tonight," added Peter, "life'll hardly be worth living."

A Battery clerk ran up, saluted and said, "Lieutenant Rutland, sir, would you please report to Major Tenet, mounted, at once."

Peter exchanged surprised glances with Tim then unpegged his horse and led it over to the Battery tent, which was already erected. Leaving his horse with a sentry he entered by the flap that the clerk was holding back for him. Major Tenet, who was now looking very ill, was standing by a table on which was spread a large basic map. Peter saluted as he neared the table.

"Ah, Peter, come and look at this," the Major wheezed as he leaned on the table. "Don't say anything just look." Peter moved towards the table, surprised by the instruction.

The map was marked with red crayon showing the salient points. On the bottom of the sheet was written 'Column'. A vertical line up the sheet was marked 'Road to Kandahar'. Halfway up this line on the left was a circle around a village marked Mizani and in the right of the line wiggled contours indicated hills close by.

"Come outside," instructed the Major, who promptly picked up his helmet and walked out of the tent with Peter behind him.

When outside the Major looked about him; slowly he mounted his horse and walked it up the road. Peter rode up to be at the Major's side.

"I've a special task for you," Tenet spoke quietly. "The column is being held up by a fortified village called Mizani, you saw its position on the map. The road is overlooked by the steep rocks on the right for about four miles, and the village and hills on the left. The fort is strong and well manned, and the natives intend to fight. General Roberts can afford no delay so he's organised an attack tomorrow morning. He's only told me and the Colonel of the Seaforths about it. Secrecy is essential with all these natives in the lines."

During this time the two men had ridden forward alongside the column towards the head.

"I'm not going to point but I want you to casually notice the features in front of you. You can see in the distance the fortified village and how it controls the passage of the road, but also note that the ground this side isn't as steep as on the roadside. A number of Seaforths will climb that slope tonight, and take the fort at dawn. Now to the left, half a mile further away from the road, is a hill that is slightly higher than the village. You're to reach the top tonight and position yourself behind the enemy and on the Seaforth's flank. You must be directly in line with the rising sun. You'll be invisible to the tribesmen in the fort, and able to fire at the inside of the defended wall. Can you see those features and appreciate what is required?"

"Yes, sir, is there an obvious track up the hill for us to follow?"

"We think so. The cavalry are reconnoitring on both sides of the main road. After the action you'll take your section down the valley between your hill and the village where there is a dried up storm river bed which you'll follow..." he paused as though short of breath. "After about three miles it joins the main road which the column will be using as soon as the Seaforths enter the village. If the tribesmen run out the back door and find you, you'll be very vulnerable to attack. Any questions?"

"When will I be able to see the cavalry report?"

"I expect 'em to return within the next couple of hours. I'll call you as soon as their report is available. Now we'll return to the Battery."

As they rode back Peter asked, "How are you feeling, sir?"

"Oh don't worry about me, my boy. I'm too old a war horse to fall by the wayside." Tenet smiled but he was looking gaunt and there was no sparkle in his eyes.

Having ridden back to the Battery tent with the Major, Peter saluted and walked back to the horse lines where he left his mount with the duty groom.

By the time he arrived at his tent he had decided how the section would leave the column with little obvious notice. "Sergeant Hills," Peter called.

"Sir." The sergeant marched over and saluted.

"Sergeant, our section will be fed first this evening and none of the men'll be required for guard duty."

"Very good, sir." Hills guessed something special was in the offing, that he would be told at the correct time, and that the men were not to be told or they would start gossiping. Hills was the backbone of the British Army; the steadfast reliable Sergeant.

As dusk fell Peter spoke to Sergeant Hills. "Are we ready to move?"

"Yes, sir, all present and correct. The men've been told to travel dead silent."

"Well done." Peter walked back down the line to Sergeant Farrant, whose gun crew were waiting the order to move.

"Single file. March," Peter called softly. The order was passed man to man down the section line; the gun crews moved off to their first night action. Anticipation, nerves and excitement knotting the stomachs and quickening the senses.

The nullah, which the cavalry had marked, was eight feet at its deepest, with a shale bottom. It lead at right angles away from the camped Field Force column running parallel to the line of hills. Feeling their way the section moved slowly down it to flank their objective.

It was amazing how much noise was still coming from the line of 20 mules and 30 gunners. Though there was no sound from the men, and the little noise from their carefully placed boots – there was always the jinkety-jink of the mules and their equipment. Peter had decided not to bring his sword; it was sure to be an encumbrance in climbing and certainly a source of noise.

A quarter of a mile later the gunners, having reached the end of this small valley, turned right towards the hills across undulating ground that was dotted with sparse trees, solitary or in clumps. The wispy grass, feed for the villagers' goats and fat-tailed sheep, luckily prevented too much noise being made by boot or hoof. From the village ahead could be heard the sounds of dogs, but Peter felt certain that they were not barking because of the gunners' approach.

After an hour's march the first slopes of the main hills were reached. Peter peered into the gloom and carefully checked to see it was the correct hill.

"Sergeant Hills," he quietly called.

"Sir," the Sergeant appeared at Peter's elbow.

"This is the hill that overlooks the village. I can't see a path up it though." He cupped his hands around his eyes to cut out any extra light, hoping to pierce the gloom and see the track.

"No, I can't see it from here. Sergeant, you go to the left a maximum of 500 yards and report back here. I'll take the right hand edge."

"Very good, sir."

Both men set off in the gloom to search for the track. Fifteen minutes later Peter returned to see Hills waiting there. "I've found the track, sir. It's 200 yards up on the left."

"Lead on, Sergeant."

The section moved to the path and followed it, rising slowly up to and behind the rounded dome.

Suddenly there was a low cry behind him; Peter turned round. A knot of gunners was standing around a man lying on the ground. He scrambled back past the laden mules. Sergeant Hills was bending over a fallen gunner and speaking to him. "If you ever let a mule tread on your ankle again, Charman, I'll leave you to the Afghan women, an' any bits they leave I'll treat very nasty." The Sergeant's voice was quiet and incisive. "Now move you 'orrible man, an' move silent like a shadder."

Peter pushed back past the gunners up to the front of the line and waved the section forward.

It was very difficult to know how far they should go into the hills before rising up the slope to the top. Eventually he decided that they would stop just below the ridge and wait for dawn. He hoped that any errors of distance, too far or too near, could be overcome by alteration on the guns. That was assuming he could find the village.

"Wait here, Sergeant. I think dawn is only a couple of hours away; the men can rest where they are. I'm just going to the crest to check our position."

Very carefully he climbed to the top of the ridge and, lying flat on the rocky ground, peered into the murky night.

The village was not actually visible but the general undulations in front of him seemed to be correct for his position. He could see the flatness of the country to his right, and he could just make out the column on the road. He felt certain that he was in the correct place. Silently he returned to the section where Hills had posted sentries while the remainder of the men huddled down in the rocks trying to keep warm in the freezing night air.

Chapter 12

In the early dim light of just before dawn the screw guns were assembled and were waiting to be wheeled into their sites. Peter again crawled up to the skyline and saw to his satisfaction that they were indeed in the correct position, there was the town below him, and through his field glasses he could see some small movement of the inhabitants at the wall furthest from him. They were manning the embrasures ready for the easy target practice that they expected, shooting down at the column as it pushed its way through the pass.

Through the gloom Peter inspected the walls at either side of the town. The main entrance and road were to the right-hand side. He could not see any sign of the Highlanders who, if they were there, were well hidden. On the left the walls merged in with the rocks but the back wall of the village was built on a rocky slope that formed the other side of the near valley; below the wall were two small squat hovels.

God it was cold! He blew onto his fingers and again examined the target area preparing the fire orders in his mind. The range would be about 1200 yards but any over-shoot shells would not be spottable, as they would fall in the valley beyond. He decided that the guns would start at 1100 yards and creep up if necessary.

Peter worried about the exact position for the guns to fire from. The sun must be directly behind them for up to fifteen minutes. Crawling back from the edge of the hill, he quietly called to the shape of a nearby gunner, "Give me your bayonet."

The gunner unsheathed his sword bayonet and handed it to Peter who stuck it vertically in the ground in front of him. If the shadow appeared slightly to the left, the guns were correctly positioned; if the first shadow appeared on the right then they must move the guns 100 yards further over. He waited in the grey light, feeling the cold getting through to him now after the exertion of the climb and the sleepless night.

It's on the right! A faint shadow appeared on the right hand side of the bayonet. Peter scrambled back to Sergeant Hills and softly said, "Move the guns 100 yards ahead. Action right."

Mumbled orders buzzed around and the gunners threw their weight onto the ropes and wheels dragging the guns to follow Peter who had run up to the new selected position. He crouched below the skyline and indicated to the Numbers 1 their specific gun sites. It took only a few minutes to move and reposition the pieces but by that time the sun had risen to give its full low-angled light over the whole area.

"Number 1 Gun ranging. Common shell 1100 yards," Peter called out the fire order in subdued tones.

The bustling activity around Number 1 gun ended and Sergeant Hills raised his arm to indicate that his piece was ready.

"Fire!" called Peter and raised his glasses to watch the fall of shot in the village.

"Fire!" shouted Hills. The screw gun barked and instantly disappeared in a cloud of white smoke.

Seconds later the 7-pound shell exploded on a house roof just inside the village. Not far enough but in the correct line for the wall.

"Number 2 gun 1150 yards. Fire." Sergeant Farrant bent down and altered the range graduation on the sights. He aimed with care, then stood up and shouted, "Fire."

This time the shell exploded with a puff of smoke close to the aiming point. The section would fire at that range and adjust any position later. Villagers were running around presumably in chaos; the screw gunners' position was invisible to them because of the blinding light of the rising sun.

"Section, 3 rounds Common shell. Fire." Number 1 gun boomed and was shortly followed by Number 2 gun. With each gun firing every thirty seconds, the village front wall was not a healthy place to be as the shells steadily slammed into the buildings close by.

Peter, watching the fall of the shells and the start of the infantry attack, noticed a bright pinprick of light appear at one of the hovels outside of the wall. A sparkle of sunlight caught the bayonets of the advancing infantry who had risen from the rocks to the low right.

Suddenly, with a boom of thunder, a gaping hole appeared in the wall in front of the advancing soldiers. Their sapper party had successfully blown a breach in the main gate for the attackers to enter.

"Left section. Cease fire."

Again the sparkle of light from the hovel caught Peter's eye; he called out to Sergeant Hills, "Section Limber up."

The Highlanders were now well into the village but rather surprisingly they did not seem to be meeting much resistance; in fact there were very few tribesmen in the village. The infantry should be able to secure it easily in the next few minutes.

The gunners swiftly dismantled and packed the screw guns onto the mules. Peter continued to watch the action in the village. A bugle call, obviously from the Seaforths, rang through the mountain air to inform the column down in the valley that the village had been secured.

The sparkle of light from the hovel caught his eye yet again and he turned his glasses down towards it. A woman was outside tottering about, picking up stones and dropping them; in her hand she had something, which she kept moving to flash in the sun.

"Ready to move, sir," Sergeant Hills reported.

"Right, Sergeant. File lead, down the trail ahead. No risks mind but we must be speedy."

Hills shouted orders to the section. In single file they prodded their mules into a brisk walk down the slope and the narrow track. Peter inspected the village once more through his glasses; it was a bustle of khaki sun helmets with the odd tribesman scampering away down the slope. But even these few could be trouble, Peter thought, if they decided to snipe at us when we get down into the valley.

The woman was still outside the hovel and Peter saw that the rocks she had dropped were making a pattern. They looked like a + with an x over the top. They almost made the pattern of – a Union Flag! The woman, who still flashed the sun's rays off the shiny object, suddenly tore off her head-cover and revealed – golden hair! My God, thought Peter, she's English!

He turned and scrambled over the rocky ground towards the moving section. Catching up with the rear mule he pushed his way down the line until he reached Sergeant Hills. Out of breath he gestured to the valley and thrust the field glasses into the Sergeant's hands.

"Down there – hovel – Englishwoman!" he gasped.

Hills peered through the glasses and said, "My goodness, you're right, sir."

"Sergeant, I'll take two men straight down the slope and meet you down the valley where the trail meets. Don't wait for me if I'm not in sight, carry on to the rendezvous with the column," he gasped.

"Right, sir," mumbled Hills still looking through the glasses. "But I think the lady's in trouble. Two men coming down the rocks above 'er." Without the binoculars Peter could see two figures running down the slope after the woman.

"Powell! Gunner Powell!" he yelled. "Here with your rifle at once."

"'Osp," Sergeant Hills called to a near gunner. "Get yer carbine – and go with Lieutenant Rutland."

Gunner Powell trotted up to Peter. "Powell, shoot those two men, then follow me down the hill. Hosp," he called, "Come with me."

Officer and gunner scrambled, fell and slid through the shale and rocks down towards the valley bottom. It was going to be a close race between the two gunners and the fleet-footed tribesmen but they were chasing a fleeing quarry. The woman was running and sliding down the opposite bank towards the tumble of rocks at the valley bottom.

The sharp stinging crack of Powell's Martini Henry ripped through the air above them, and Peter saw the leading Afghan stumble, then roll down the slope. The second tribesman hardly slowed but ran sure-footedly down past the fallen man. Peter could see that he had a jezail in one hand and a curved sword in the other. He was only slowly closing on the fleeing woman, and was jumping from side to side in a zigzag fashion.

Again Powell's rifle cracked and the man fell but instantly rose, and without picking up his jezail, ran straight towards the blonde woman with his sword held high. Peter and Hosp were only a few yards from the valley bottom when the Afghan caught up with the girl. He slashed at her back with the curved blade but just missed; as he raised the blade again Powell's third shot hit him. The heavy slug slammed into his chest throwing him backwards onto the rocks despite his downward run. Hosp, who was slightly ahead of Peter, scrambled across the dried up riverbed and reached the girl. He caught hold of her arm and looked round for orders.

"Straight on down the valley," Peter gasped.

The three of them set off scrambling over small boulders and around large rocks that obviously formed the bed of a torrential river when the snows melted.

Peter took off his sun helmet as he ran. He was already soaked with sweat and the perspiration was streaming off his face. Hosp, still helmeted and carrying a carbine, was helping the girl along when necessary.

The sharp crack of a Martini made Peter look up. Powell had moved about 100 yards down the trail but had then stopped to shoot at the opposite valley face where a further two or three tribesmen had taken up the chase.

Peter turned to scramble after the gunner and the girl who were now well ahead. God, he thought, one slip – one broken bone and we've had it. There was no sign of the troop nor where the trail would meet the valley bottom but he knew that the three of them could not keep up this pace for much longer.

The Martini's crack sounded again; Peter stopped and quickly but deliberately scanned the town side of the valley. How close was the pursuit and how many?

Eight was the how many, Powell had just stopped the ninth but they were running on the smooth ground on the sides of the valley and were managing to close very quickly. He decided to make a stand.

"Gunner Hosp," he shouted towards the couple that were 20 yards in front of him. "Stand fast!" and he threw himself over boulders to reach them.

"Get down," he told the girl. "Hosp – shoot who you can. I'll use my revolver for when they get close." The gunner pulled at his pouch flap and placed a round in the carbine breech. Actions so obviously the result of long hours of drilled training. He knelt on his right knee, snapped shut the action and aimed – a good deliberate aim – at the middle of the nearest man. CRACK! Butt down, action open, eject spent cartridge, place in new round, close breech, aim.

By this time the remaining seven were only 80 yards away and Peter thought about trying his revolver when from high up behind them, Powell's rifle reduced the enemy by yet another one. Hosp fired again and a running tribesman fell to his knees then rose and, holding his side, staggered away from the action.

A group of three men were closing fast on the left, presumably the other two were coming up the riverbed. Resting the butt of his heavy Enfield revolver on a large rock, Peter aimed at the leading man of the three. Bang! The bullet missed, kicking up shale and dust behind the target. A distant crack preceded the leading Afghan's death-fall as Powell notched up yet another score. A loud crack from Hosp's carbine felled the second man; the third tribesman threw himself to the ground and scrambled behind cover.

But where were the original two who had broken away from the group?

"Hosp. Fix your bayonet," Peter called. "Two more men in the rocks in front."

There was a scrambling noise in the far rocks. The survivor of the left-hand group was running back towards the village, unhurt but scared. Hosp fired at the running figure but missed. We can't stay here for long, thought Peter. Where are they?

The girl pulled at his arm. "Look!"

A flutter of cloth showed on his right as with a high-pitched scream of "Allah Akba!" a large white-clad figure with raised sword, appeared on a large rock above Hosp. The native's sword blade swept down – no time to load, just reflex drill – bayonet parry and lunge. The gunner's rifle barrel thudded up against the Afghan's chest and a spike of bayonet stood out of his back. The tribesman's sword sliced down onto the gunner's helmet, splitting it, but the blade was deflected; it slewed away from Hosp's head, and bit deeply into his shoulder.

Peter thrust his revolver into his holster and scrambled towards the wounded gunner.

"Another one!" screamed the girl pointing over Peter's shoulder.

The last tribesman had silently appeared from the tumbled rock, and was now only ten paces away. He did not run. He was walking steadily towards Peter with his sword held high.

Peter groped for this revolver but the lanyard had tangled with his belt – the muzzle would not come clear of the holster. Just a few paces away, the large Afghan with the sword held above his head let a smile break through the bearded face. Then with a jerk Peter freed the cumbersome Enfield handgun, and snatched a shot at the looming figure. The heavy slug slammed into the tribesman's head. The force threw him bodily to the ground; he had died in a jihad – the smile still on his lips – he was now with his God. Peter lurched to his feet and looked around to see if any more hill men were about. "Hell that was close!" Keeping his revolver in his hand he went over to the wounded Hosp who was holding his left arm.

"How are you?"

"Alright, sir."

"No he's not," interjected the girl, "He's bleeding badly. Get his jacket off and I'll bind him up." Not questioning this direct order, Peter holstered his revolver and unbuckled Hosp's equipment, then gently removed his jacket. The girl tore strips from her underskirt and with these she swiftly and efficiently bound up the gunner's shoulder. The dressing seemed to staunch the flow of blood; it also immobilised his arm.

"Help me get his jacket on," she ordered.

Peter picked up the carbine and helped Hosp to his feet. "I'll help him," the girl said as she pulled the gunner's good arm over her shoulder.

"Right, straight down the valley but we'll go along the lower slope on the left side, it looks easier than the river bed," Peter instructed.

Hosp and the girl staggered towards the slope. Peter heard a call from above him and looked up. It was Powell. He was shouting then pointing down the valley; his rifle slung on his shoulder. Obviously there were no more tribesmen pursuing them. Peter breathed a sigh of relief.

He was about to start after the other two when he saw the tulwar sword still in the hand of the Afghan he had shot. It was a beautifully engraved blade that seemed to shine; the large hand-guard was of gold and silver inlay with stones. A sword might be useful later on. He tried to pull it from the dead hand but he found that the fingers were still gripping the hilt quite tightly. Peter looked at the tribesmen's head and saw that the revolver bullet had not killed him but had glanced along the skull above the left ear. The big man was obviously still alive but unconscious. Peter jerked the sword out of the reflex grip then, holding it and Hosp's carbine, he ran to catch up with the wounded gunner.

After half an hour Hosp was seriously weakening from the loss of blood, though he staggered on without complaint; his taut, grey face told of his pain. The girl was on his right side with her arm around his waist, her hand locked into his belt. Peter could do little to assist as the wounded shoulder precluded assistance for the gunner on his left side; Peter went ahead hoping to catch sight of the section. He rounded a small shoulder in the hillside and saw, half a mile ahead of them, the section's mules that had almost reached the bottom of the valley.

Peter scrambled up a rock and, waving the carbine above his head shouted at the top of his voice, "Sergeant Hills!"

He could see faces turn round towards him and they section stopped. The girl looked all in, while Hosp's eyes were closed and he was obviously about to collapse.

"Let me take him now," Peter told the girl and drew Hosp's right arm onto his shoulder to give maximum assistance.

The Sergeant, seeing that help was needed, had sent back two stalwart gunners who instantly picked up the injured man, and carried him towards the guns. They willingly helped but there was no obvious sympathy.

"Wotcha been doin' 'ospy?"

"Always fort you 'ad a chip on yer shoulder, now you've gotta chip in it." But Hosp was too near unconsciousness to respond to these quips.

By the time they reached the section Sergeant Hills had already reorganised the loads so that the wounded gunner could be carried on a mule. The girl asked for proper bandages to replace the blood-soaked rags and then she bound up the terrible wound more effectively.

"Sergeant, arrange for this lady to be carried as well as Hosp, will you," ordered Peter.

"Yes, sir," replied Hills.

"No. I'll walk, and my name is Beatrice Nashton, and thank you for rescuing me."

Peter smiled at the tumble of words. "Not at all, Miss Nashton, it was our pleasure but don't you think you are too tired to walk?"

"Why? I have walked from Kabul to Samangan and back again. I'll stay with Gunner Hosp, his wound might start to bleed again."

Sergeant Hills spoke quietly to Peter. "Excuse me, sir, but 'osp said that 'e won't ride a mule, he'd rather walk, so we've made a litter for 'im. The lads'll carry it, sir."

"Thank you, Sergeant. It's probably for the best. Right we must move off at once."

Chapter 13

The section, with two gunners well in front to act as scouts, picked its way down the rocky track that ran alongside the dried-up river bed. Just over one mile ahead the steep-sided valley swung sharply to the right. The track should join up with the main road to Kandahar just around the bend.

The temperature had not risen to its roasting fullness; in fact it was quite pleasant strolling along in the morning sun. Peter was walking at the head of the line of mules talking to Sergeant Hills.

"We must be well ahead of the Field Force on the main road," he said. "We'll push on and have a rest while we wait for them on the main road. I'll…" he stopped and lifted his hand. The two scouting gunners, who were one hundred yards ahead of the section, had stopped and were crouching down.

"Halt the section, Sergeant."

Hills turned and signalled to the line of guns to halt; one of the scouts was running back bending low, while the other gunner stayed crouching behind a boulder.

"What's the trouble, Hoskins?"

"Tribesmen, sir, 'undreds of them all sittin' down just up the road a bit."

"Sergeant, keep the men quiet. I'm going to have a look."

Peter and Gunner Hoskins trotted forward keeping low until they were close to the boulder, then they crawled the last few yards. Carefully he peered round the large rock. The sharp bend in the valley and the junction with the road was only a few hundred yards away. Inside the valley, just short of the road, was a large gathering of tribesmen. Most of them were squatting on their haunches while the rest stood but all of them were silently facing towards the junction. Carefully counting one group he multiplied up. "My God, there's about two hundred of them!"

"It looks like an ambush, sir."

"Yes for the main column." He backed slowly away.

"Bryant, stay here but don't be seen. Keep low and still. Hoskins, come with me."

Again officer and gunner crawled away and then scurried back to the section. "It looks nasty, Sergeant. There's about two hundred Afghans ready to ambush the column. Thank goodness they haven't seen us. They're all intently looking towards the road."

"That's why the village was empty, sir. They're all in the big ambush. Can we attack them and warn the column?"

"No, if the enemy turned on us we'd easily be overrun, and we'd lose the guns."

Peter looked up the valley towards the ambush position. The problem was to push the Afghans out into the road in front of the column that must be warned of the imminent attack. But how?

Standing in the middle of the road, hands on hips, a plan started to slowly form in his mind. Through his binoculars he scanned the right-hand side of the valley and the rock edge further forward. Yes, it could work.

"Sergeant, both guns to be assembled by Numbers 1 to 4. Sergeant Farrant to be in charge. The rest of the gunners and all of the drivers to have carbines and 30 rounds of ammunition each."

Hills turned to Farrant standing close by, "'Ear that, Charlie?"

"Yes, Sarge."

"Then do it."

Peter called out quietly, "Powell, Martins, come here."

The two gunners ran towards him, Powell holding his rifle.

"Both of you are to climb up the slope to the right, near that scrubby tree." Peter pointed to the skyline of the ridge running between the valley and the Kandahar road. "From there you should be able to see the column. Work out how far they are from the position then, Martins, you come back and report to me. Powell, I am sure you can't get down the other side but if you can report to Major Tenet. If you can't get down you will stay hidden and wait until the leading cavalry patrol is directly below you then fire three rounds into the ground in front of them. You mustn't be seen by the patrol, then come down the slope and help us. Understand?"

"Yes, sir."

"Then be off." The two men trotted across the valley floor and started to scramble up the scree and tumbled rocks.

The two assembled screw guns stood ready in the middle of the track. To move them forwards over the rough ground would be very difficult for the four gunners but that was all he could spare. Hills was issuing carbines and ammunition to the rest of the gunners. Ammo pouches and pockets were bulging; 30 rounds was more than the usual issue for the carbines.

"Sergeant Farrant," Peter called. "Get me a dozen cartridges for the guns and something to carry them in." He felt in his pockets for matches. One box with only three matches in it.

"I want two boxes of matches," he called out to the group of men near to Sergeant Hills. He selected a couple from the numerous hands held out to him, and put them into his pocket.

He looked forward towards the ambush area where Bryant was still kneeling down watching the tribesmen. So far so good. Peter slowly went through the plan details in his mind. It might just work.

"Will this do, sir?" Farrant held a mule's feedbag with twelve of the pound-and-a-half gunpowder cartridges. The feed strap would go over his shoulder.

"Yes that's fine."

In a cloud of dust and a clatter of rocks Gunner Martins slithered back onto the track and ran over to report. "The column's about 'alf a mile away, sir."

"Good. Can Powell get down?"

"No, sir, the cliff's as straight as a beggar can spit."

"Sarn't Hills, Sarn't Farrant, here please." The two men stood in the circling dust in front of Peter.

"We must make the tribesmen think that a massive force is coming down the valley, and they can only escape out onto the road. This is what I want you to do."

Carefully he explained his plan. Not surprisingly neither of the Sergeants looked overjoyed at the idea but it seemed the only way out.

"Any questions? Then start moving." Peter swung the feedbag over his shoulder; he caught sight of the girl standing by the stretcher with the wounded gunner.

"Miss Nashton, will you stay in the rocks with Hosp. If we are overrun I suggest you try and get up the slope towards the gunner with the rifle."

"I'll stay with Hosp."

"You will not stay with him. If the tribesmen get past the guns you will go up the slope."

"And Hosp?"

"He will shoot himself. Now please get into those rocks."

"Here's a carbine for you, sir," Hills held out the stubby weapon.

"No. I'll take the Afghan sword and my revolver." He felt the small revolver ammunition pouch on the back of his belt; it was full with ten rounds.

He scrambled up the right-hand side of the valley and moved slowly forwards towards the ambush area. After a few minutes climbing, with the sweat pouring off him, he could see the first of the tribesmen kneeling and waiting on the valley floor below. Still climbing and moving forward he passed the position of the forward lookout gunner below. He had to move with care, as the scree was difficult to cross without sending a cascade down the slope to the track below.

Slowly and with great care, he crawled on hand and knees for the last fifty yards, hiding behind rocks and scrub until he was above the ambush and could even see the valley entrance to the Kandahar road. On the slope in front of him were some large boulders lodged on the hillside. Slowly he slid towards one and carefully pushed one of the powder cartridges into a crevice underneath it. He tamped the charge in with sand and rocks leaving a small part of the cartridge showing. This he pierced with the tip of the tulwar sword. He cut a hole on another of the cartridges and gently poured out a train of powder away from the primed rock. After twenty yards he selected two more large boulders that he also charged with a cartridge underneath each one. He joined these cartridges together to the same powder trail.

Down below in the valley the two screw guns had been pulled up the track towards the forward lookout. They would only have ten or fifteen yards to move before they could fire at the tribesmen.

Peter plugged another of the charges into a large scree slide, hoping it might give off masses of dust as the loose boulders fell; it might even start a big rock slide. He pushed in three more charges before he exhausted the powder. Some of the charges were on a common trail while others were on individual fuses. He hoped to detonate them at different times.

Having finished, he sat down behind some scrub, and wiped the sweat from his face. He undid the flap of his revolver holster, and then took out a box of matches. He held the tulwar sword and the box in his left hand and a match ready to strike in his right.

Now we wait.

He could see below on the rocky slope, Sergeant Hills kneeling down with the gunners holding their carbines. They

were ready to run into position as soon as they heard
Powell's shots.

It might work; it will certainly give the Afghans a hell of a
shock but will... What the Hell!

He shielded his eyes with his hands. My God it was Hosp
and the girl. Both of them were staggering down the track;
she was helping him limp along while he held a carbine in his
free hand.

Crack!

Crack!

Crack!

The distinct reports of Powell's rifle ripped through the
air. Peter struck a match and put the burning head onto two
of the powder trails. One would explode under three separate
rocks while the other would explode on the scree.

The powder trail fizzed and crackled agonisingly slowly
across the sand.

In the valley the two screw guns, with only half crews,
were being madly heaved over the rocky track. They turned
the corner – the gunners spun the guns to face the Afghans –
cartridges and shells were rammed home then the crews knelt
down – and waited.

Sergeant Hills and his men raced out and up the slope the
moment they heard Powell's shots. They scrambled behind
rocks and scrub, loaded their carbines, took aim – and
waited.

Some of the tribesmen turned round on hearing the sound
of the shots but even those who saw the movement behind
them did not appear concerned.

The powders trails smokily fizzed and spluttered along.
God they seemed to take ages.

BOOM!

BAWOOM!

An ever-widening shower of rock splinters tore into the
air followed by a massive cloud of tumbling dust. One of the

large boulders was dislodged. Gradually it built up speed to career down the slope towards the ambush.

Bang! The first screw gun fired while the echo of the main explosion was still ripping around the valley. The rattle of the gunners firing their carbines was almost lost in the roaring cacophony of the explosions. Each man fired off five rounds as quickly as he could, then followed the ten carefully aimed shots.

WHUMP! The charge in the scree thumped out. The results were spectacular but hardly dangerous. A roar of small rocks tumbled down the hillside, each one creating its own swirling dust storm. In the blinding cloud Peter ran forward and struck matches to set off the other two trails.

Bang! The other screw gun fired. They were firing at fifteen-second intervals to keep up a steady hail of metal howling into the enemy. The noise and the clouds of dust plus the thunder of the falling rocks were successfully spreading panic through the Afghans.

Peter, his eyes smarting, scrambled back through the dust then slid down the valley side towards his guns. It must have worked! It must have worked! They must be pouring out onto the main road!

Bang! A gun barked again, and disappeared into a cloud of white gun smoke.

From halfway down Peter could see a large number of Afghans running towards the junction – but through the dust on the slopes he noticed a cluster of fifty or more tribesmen dodging through the rocks towards the guns.

"Over to your right! Fire over to the right!" but Sergeant Farrant could not hear the orders over the all-enveloping noise.

Bang! A gun fired again down the track probably hitting no one at all.

Peter, waving his sword above his head, slid down the slope towards the guns. The screening dust cloud that had terrified the main body of Afghans was now a perfect cover for the smaller group to advance under. The gunners with their carbines could only see the wall of dust, while the guns slammed their shells into this blinding screen.

"Hold your fire! Hold your fire! Sergeant Hills, hold your fire!"

BOOM. Another powder charge threw rocks and boulders into the air further down the valley. More dust, more confusion.

"There are tribesmen creeping up under the dust. Hold your fire until you see them," Peter yelled out to both the sergeants. The two men acknowledged. Farrant loaded the second gun – and again they waited. An uncanny quiet fell on the position. The dust curtain swirled gently one way then the other in the light breeze. It was as thick as a London fog; in some places you could only see a few feet in front.

Then came the terrible Afghan war scream. Swelling up from nothing, it filled the dust-laden air of the whole valley. The sound keened around the gunners turning their blood cold as the terrible sound ripped through the swirling fog.

"Down the track. They're down the track. Fire."

"NO!"

Bang! Number 2 gun fired but the near rocks sent the metal ricocheting away. Some of the gunners with carbines could see the enemy now. They started shooting hard and fast but gunners are notoriously bad riflemen. The warrior tribesmen kept on coming. Strangely none was shooting; a large group only twenty yards away were visible for a few seconds through the swirling dust.

Peter stood up beside Number 1 gun, pulled out his revolver and carefully fired six shots; he holstered the gun and waving the tulwar above his head shouted out to the section. "Steady, gunners. The infantry will be with us soon. Steady." He faced down the track. If they're not coming soon we're done for.

The dust cloud swirled closer in, then suddenly it cleared. Five Afghans to his right were sprinting towards him. The first man fell as a carbine bullet smashed into him. The next one came charging on a spear, held like a lance, straight in front of him. Peter raised the blade of the tulwar ready for the downward slash – but the warrior slowed down in his charge. The spear point dropped. He called out and pointed at Peter. The following man also stopped and shouted. Then both men turned and, giving a weird shrieking yell, ran back into the dust cloud. Gradually the other tribesmen turned and followed seemingly in a daze as they retreated back onto the swirling cloud of dust and gun smoke.

Chapter 14

"Blimey they've scarpered."

Mabbs' Cockney voice rose above the crackling of the carbines.

"Cease fire," Peter yelled to the men on the screw guns.

"Sergeant Hills, hold your fire." He repeated the order to the men on the hillside.

Gradually the smoke and dust drifted away like a fine net curtain, revealing the small valley and the junction with the main road. The gunners could see a company of Ghurkhas, who were spread across the riverbed and slowly advancing.

Peter stood between the guns, the tulwar sword still in his hands. Why did they turn? They had almost overrun us, and they stopped. Why? He shook his head at the crazy idea that formed in his mind. It was time to rejoin the Field Force.

"Limber up. Sergeant Hills, let me know our losses."

The gunners slid and scampered down the slopes to dismantle the mountain pieces.

"Sergeant, where can I find the bandages?" Miss Nashton called.

"Jones get the dressings pack off that mule for the lady," Sergeant Hills replied and then turned to Peter. "Three men dead, five wounded, sir."

The wounded gunners were being bandaged and tended by Miss Nashton with such expertise that it was obvious she had done this work before, if not under these conditions.

Peter felt dazed; his mind was in turmoil. He looked at the sword still in his hand. The bright gems sparkled at him while the bright damascened blade reflected the sunlight like a mirror. Could it be that the sword had stopped the Ghazi charge?

Sergeant Hills marched up, stood before him and reported. "Left Section is limbered up, sir. Of the five wounded only Gunner Epps can't walk; well 'e says 'e can't because 'es got a lump out of 'is leg. The rest of the men are bandaged up, thanks to the lady, and ready to go."

"Right, Sergeant. I'll report to the Surgeon to arrange transport for Epps. Who were the men killed?"

Hills took out his field notebook and slowly read out the names. He closed the book, placed it in his pocket and said, "The lady said that 'osp saved 'er life sir. Used 'is carbine one-handed and killed two of them."

Peter looked over to where Hosp was lying on the stretcher with Miss Nashton kneeling over him. The girl looked up as he walked towards the wounded gunner.

"This man deserves a medal. He made me get him a gun with a bayonet and some bullets. He sat against that rock and fired his gun with one hand, and when an Afghan tried to hit me with a sword he dug his bayonet in him and he fell on him and died. He saved my life."

Peter smiled at the rush of words telling the garbled story. He knelt down beside the wounded man who was now looking very ill. "Well done, Hosp."

"The lady means a carbine sir not a gun."

"I rather gathered that. Well done." The words were so inadequate; he put his hand on the gunner's unwounded shoulder and gave it a squeeze. God! With men like this who are willing to fight and die, Victoria will never lose her empire, he thought.

He stood up and walked over to Sergeant Hills who had already organised the move back into the column marching along the road to Kandahar.

After the midday halt, Peter decided to ride down the column so that he could visit the wounded men. One or two of the old sweats were obviously making the most of being carried on horseback or in the dandies; anything was better than regimental duties or fatigues, so they milked their wounds to the greatest amount. Gunner Hosp was looking very ill but the Surgeon was sure that as long as he did not break his dressing again, recovery would be straightforward. Peter spurred his horse to canter up to the section again when he saw Miss Nashton riding close to the Surgeon's section. He trotted over to her and drew his horse alongside of hers.

"How are you now, Miss Nashton?"

"Very well thank you, Lieutenant, but please my name is Bee – short for Beatrice."

"Mine is Peter."

"So I found out from your men. They think a great deal of you."

He smiled. "I hope you won't think me impertinent but what on earth were you doing in that hovel below the village?"

"Such consideration and politeness," Bee laughed; she put her hand to her mouth. "I'm sorry, I'm not laughing at you but, after the way I've been treated over the past few months, I find such gentlemanly actions unusual and rather amusing. Now I'm being pompous – forgive me."

She turned her face towards him with her head slightly tilted; her bright looks seemed to shine at him.

"I haven't yet thanked you for saving me," she continued, "You and Gunner Hosp were like two knights in shining armour as you seemed to fly down that slope towards me. Oh I was so frightened." She reached across and put her hand on his, which was resting on the pommel of his saddle. "But you want the story from the beginning."

"Only if you feel up to it."

"Well my father is – or was – a missionary for the Methodist Evangelical Society. My mother died five years ago, and for the past year or so I have been travelling with Father through the Punjab towards Islamabad. I've always wanted to become a Doctor but I couldn't leave Father."

She spoke in a low voice as she reluctantly recalled the sad, recent past.

"We joined up with the Mission that was to be led by Sir Louis Cavagnari. I begged Father not to go into Afghanistan where it is obvious that Christianity is the last thing that they want to be taught. The native faith in the Muslim religion is fanatical, as you saw yesterday when they attacked your guns. But whatever I said, Father knew better, so we joined the mission to Kabul. Because we both speak Pushtu we were able to live in a house close to the Embassy. When the Amir's soldiers attacked it they weren't aware of us but my poor father went out to reason with them – with a Bible in his hand." Bee gave a sob and her voice trailed away as she hung her head. Peter could see the tears on her cheeks. He continued to ride beside her as she silently wept.

"His faith was just as strong as theirs; he was so brave but they cut him down, and laughed – oh God how they laughed."

Peter could hardly hear her speak as she turned her head away from him to face the rocky wilderness they were riding through. Her shoulders shook as she silently sobbed out her grief for the dead father she loved – foolhardy but so brave.

The horses continued their steady plod, remaining in position in the column with Peter saying nothing, just waiting for Bee's anguish to fade away. She fumbled for her handkerchief, wiped her eyes, composed herself and continued her story.

"I tried to stay hidden in the house but when the Embassy had fallen and all those brave Guides were killed, the Afghans started searching for anyone who had collaborated with the British. They found me early one morning and I was dragged into the square in front of the Consulate where a dozen wretched Afghans were huddled together. Presumably they'd helped Cavagnari, or at least were supposed to have helped him in some way. I was the only European, in fact the only woman. We were surrounded by a mob of 50 or 60 armed men who were shouting at us. Occasionally another poor wretch was thrown into our group, and we found a common bond in huddling together. The mob, though not very large, was beginning to chant some phrase rhythmically, and I could feel that they were working themselves up to a climax.

"Then I decided that, as I was definitely going to be killed, I wouldn't die huddled together with the terrified natives. I thought of my brave father and I pushed my way clear of the crowd and stood slightly apart from them. The chanting was now louder. To help quieten my terror I closed my eyes and recited the 23rd Psalm to myself. I'd almost finished it when I realised that the chanting had stopped. The crowd had opened up a large gap and there stood a big man dressed in rich clothes. He spoke to a guard standing bedside him, who walked up to me and said something that I didn't understand. He then spoke in Pushtu, and said 'Come with me.' He led me to the large man in the crowd who silently looked me up and down then turned and walked back through the crowd who parted out of his way. As I was led along I decided that the big man was not doing all this just to kill me, so I presumed that he wanted his way with me – a fate worse than death."

Bee gave a bitter laugh. "But that was not to be." She turned to Peter, "I am very thirsty, do you have some water?"

He pulled his canteen from his saddlebag, removed the cork and handed it to her. As she raised the container to her lips and drank, he looked at her profile and thought – what a remarkable woman.

She lowered the canteen, wiped the spout with her hand and replaced the cork. It was not a feminine action; it might have been a fellow officer who was sharing Peter's water bottle. Still holding the container on her lap, she continued her story. "Looking back I think that I was to be used as a bargaining point, a hostage or barter. I was kept prisoner in a room in a large house in the north of Kabul near to the

Sherpur. I was fed and clothed and left alone. Then some days later there was pandemonium in the house, I could hear raised voices shouting commands and, outside in the courtyard, the sound of a number of horses on the cobbles. Suddenly the big man appeared at the door." She turned her head towards Peter. "He was the man you shot in the river bed."

"The one whose sword I took?"

"Did you? I didn't know that, there is something special about that sword, or it may be the scabbard. Anyway he spoke to me in Pushtu saying that he was my guard and that we would be travelling on a long journey. He led me out into the courtyard where a group of uniformed Afghans were seated on horses and obviously eager to move. My guard and I mounted, and we set off to ride hard for two days, until we reached a small village. From the gestures and leers of the other riders, I'm sure they had lecherous thoughts towards me but my guardian protected me with calm assurance. That night while we slept, the uniformed men disappeared, taking with them all of the supplies and the horses, including my guard's. He showed no sign of anger, just arranged for food from the villagers and we simply set off to walk to our destination – wherever that was to be.

"Eventually we reached a large town called Samangan. We stayed there a week or two. I wasn't locked up or treated as a captive but allowed to stay with the women in the kitchen to generally assist with their duties. Though I managed to converse with these women quite well, they were reluctant to tell me the name of the big man who was my guard. At first they pretended they didn't know but eventually I realised that they knew but wouldn't tell me or rather wouldn't say his name out loud. He was obviously respected and loved to the point of deification but eventually I found a girl who'd been to a mission school in Peshawar, so I asked her to tell me my guard's name. She told me he had many names, and she refused to tell me his present name, but eventually she wrote it for me in the sand. It was Talafi."

Bee stretched out her arm and returned the canteen of water to Peter.

"I began to feel that he was on some sort of pilgrimage, and walking was part of the requirements. He had a dedicated hatred of the British Army; I think they had harmed his family some time ago. This time we went south, travelling on the main road back towards Kabul, sometimes alone, other times with groups of fellow travellers. As I was able to give the occasional assistance to the odd injured or sick person, I was allowed to move freely. Talafi trusted me not to escape – not that I had anywhere to escape to."

Bee paused in her narrative, and looked around at the arid rocky scrub they were passing through. They travelled in silence for a few minutes; Peter deciding not to break into her thoughts. The dust puffed around their horses' hooves as they evenly paced along.

"We travelled for weeks, walking through the hills until two days ago we arrived at the little village where you rescued me. I was helping to milk the goats when I heard your guns. I didn't know that the Field Force was on the main road, so I could only contact you. You and your guns looked so small up in the hills, so I decided I'd catch your attention with reflecting sunlight from a shiny brass brooch I had. I couldn't call to you; then I thought of a Union flag design, and it was only as I finished and took off my head scarf to wave it that I realised my fair hair was probably the best indication of a foreigner in Afghanistan."

"You were right about that," confirmed Peter. "Your hair certainly convinced me that you were British. Incidentally your guard, Talafi, the man I shot, he isn't dead. When I picked up his sword I found that my bullet had glanced off his skull and obviously stunned him. The blood was just a bad scalp wound. I think he's alive but has a massive headache."

Bee did not speak for some time. She stared ahead over her horse's nodding head. "I'm glad that he isn't dead. There's something evil about him but also strong and fine." She faced Peter. "You say that you took his sword?"

"Yes, I'd left mine with the column, so I took his for self-defence. It appears to have some fine gems in the handle."

"There's something special about that sword," Bee said. "He always carried it covered up, wrapped in a length of soft leather. I only saw it once when we stopped at one of the villages, he uncovered it and placed it on a large stone to show it to one of the village headmen. This headman actually bowed before it and placed his head on the sand. At one time I saw Talafi use it to calmly chop off a man's hand who had been caught stealing."

Peter nodded. "That answers my query. During the Ghazi charge yesterday, when you were with Hosp, I used the sword in the fighting. I think some of the tribesmen saw it in my hand and promptly broke off the attack."

Bee smiled. "Maybe an Islamic relic actually saved some Christian lives – how strange.

Chapter 15

Twenty days after leaving Kabul, as the road crested the Momand hills, the relief column sighted Kandahar. The city was totally enclosed by a solid wall, twenty to thirty feet tall, on all four sides. Against the northern wall on the inside there was a taller walled citadel that guarded the main entrance, named the Kedgah gate. Close against the eastern wall was the bustling town of Deh-I-Khoja that consisted of a large conglomeration of low squat buildings, one or two stories high. They were made of mud bricks; the outside plastered and painted white. Many had ornate castellated edges to the roofs but all of them had shutter windows. It could be seen that from some of the open windows hung brightly patterned rugs and blankets.

Around the outer edge of the town were orchards and cultivated fields, many containing the ubiquitous goats and the local fat-tailed sheep. Beyond the cultivated areas the rock-strewn desert spread out towards the Pushti-Rud hills far to the north-west, only just visible through the dust haze.

The relief column encamped on the edge of the fields beside the town of Deh-I-Khoja. 6/8 Battery's defensive position was at the extreme edge on the higher ground leading out to the far hills.

The relieved garrison had not been under great pressure, being fully stocked with food and ammunition, and in a very strong defensive position. Ayub Khan had pulled his forces away from the city as soon as he learned of the approach of the British force, and was now encamped somewhere in the Pushti-Rud hills. Cavalry patrols were instantly sent out by General Roberts to ascertain the enemy's position and strength.

Because the defensive wall of Kandahar was intact, the garrison had been able to control the flow of natives in and out of the city. The main bazaar had fallen into disuse over the past months due to the restriction of movement, while the bazaar in the adjoining town had grown considerably. In fact it was now the main and growing centre for the commerce in the region. Kandahar's stout city walls also precluded any expansion to allow for extra occupants. This meant that the adjoining village had grown to be a significant sized town just outside the city walls.

Now that the relief column had encamped in the country around it, this town was considered to be a safe area for military personnel as obviously the natives were controllable and so considered friendly.

6/8 Battery mule lines were situated alongside a battered orchard wall that helped to shelter the animals from the scorching sun at midday and the cold winds at midnight. Tarpaulins covered the heaps of equipment that was stacked in orderly lines leading up to the Battery tents.

On arrival at Kandahar, Major Tenet was immediately taken to the Field Hospital where he was recovering from the fever that had hit him on the march. Captain Dainby had assumed command of the Battery.

On one of his regular visits to the mules, Peter was examining a saddle sore on one of the animals while Assan forked over the straw around Satan's feet.

"I have something for you, Sahib," Assan murmured, continuing his work.

Peter stopped his examination, his hand still on the mule's rump. "Something for me?"

"Yes, Sahib. I don't think it is very good." Assan worked on without looking up at Peter. "A man in the Deh-I-Khoja bazaar gave me a mug that he said was made in Rutlandshire. Is that in England, Sahib?"

"Yes it is."

Assan put a hand into his jacket top and pulled out a tin mug. He walked close to Peter, pushed it into his hand and carried on with his work. A quick look at the mug showed a piece of paper stuck inside on the bottom. Peter slipped it into his pouch and strolled out of the mule lines.

Back in his tent, Peter closely examined the tin mug and carefully pulled out the folded paper that was stuck inside the bottom. He carefully unfolded the thin sheet and spread it out onto his travelling writing pad. The writing was in English, which pleased him, but the message left him mystified. It simply said, 'Meet a sea-borne friend when the grass disappears to the crossed Christian cross.'

He carefully read the note a number of times, and then eventually deduced that the 'sea-borne friend' must be Captain Anstruther. Peter had never been on a ship before so Edward must be the friend suggested, but the rest of the message left his mind blank. He wondered if 'when the grass disappears' was where the cultivated fields met the desert area, but if so he could not work out where 'the crossed Christian cross' came in. The shape of a Christian cross was obvious; but why a crossed cross? One crossed a road, or crossed two breeds of animals, or was crossed in love – but how to cross a cross?

Then the answer hit him. Of course! The mule was a cross between two breeds, a horse and a donkey – and a donkey has a dark shaped cross on its withers and down its spine. This cross, by popular superstition, was given to the animal when it bore Jesus on Palm Sunday, and this mark could often be seen on the mules. So the instructions were to meet Anstruther in the mule lines.

'When the grass disappears.' The animals were always given cut grass late in the evening for them to eat during the night. Peter tore up the note; then he paused with his hands still holding the pieces. What was Anstruther doing in

Kandahar, and why did he want to meet in this mysterious way?

The answer came a few hours later. Peter had strolled along to the mule lines and seated himself on the Farrier Sergeant's anvil amongst the shoeing tongs and rasps. Though it was only the Battery horses that were shod, it was the farrier who examined and trimmed the mules' hooves as necessary.

Peter watched the bustle of the native muleteers as they removed the mule dung, then groomed and fed their charges, finally leaving a pile of cut grass for each mule. While he sat watching this industry, he expected some contact to be made with him – a nod of the head, a wave of the hand but he noticed nothing.

Slowly the muleteers completed their tasks, finally wandering off individually or in groups back to their quarters. As the last group left, Peter remained seated on the anvil all alone and feeling rather disappointed. Then he saw that there was one solitary muleteer still spreading some cut grass at a mule's head. Having completed his task the man shuffled his way up the lines towards Peter touching the muzzles of the mules with his hand or their grass feed with his bare foot. Peter heard the man mutter to himself. "Well I'll be damned. If it isn't the bookworm from the old *Empress of India.*"

It was Anstruther's voice but as the muleteer turned towards Peter the brown, scarred face showed that it was not Edward. Or was it?

"Hello, Peter." When the voice could be seen to be coming from the face itself, then Peter could see that it was indeed Captain Edward Anstruther.

"Edward! I never recognised you."

"That is rather the idea, old chap. How're things with you?"

"Fine, Edward. Dare I ask the same of you?"

"No time, old chap. Our meeting must be as brief and inconspicuous as possible. Walk down to the end of the orchard wall by that fallen olive tree."

Peter rose from his iron seat and strolled towards the place Edward had described. It was now dusk and in a few minutes it would be dark. A Sikh sentry standing by the wall saluted Peter as he walked by.

"Sit down by that wall," Edward instructed.

He was standing against the old gnarled olive tree only five feet away. "The sentry'll be able to see you but not me. Now tell me why do I hear your name mentioned with such enmity in Afghan circles."

"My name?"

"Yes. The comments are pure hatred, and I can't learn of any connection with the Koran. What've you done to earn this hostility?"

"Oh God. The sword," murmured Peter.

"Tell me. Concisely," Edward ordered.

Peter explained how he had obtained the sword and how the sight of it had seemed to stem the Ghazi charge.

"My God. You've stirred up a hornet's nest," said Edward. "There is precious little we can do, but your story explains some of the queries we've had. There's someone big in the Afghan camp who's very keen to kill you, of that there's no doubt."

"How about me returning the sword?" Peter suggested.

"A clean-cut English gentleman's attitude," replied Anstruther, "but the natives won't appreciate the gesture. The weapon has been dirtied by being handled by infidels. No they won't accept it back."

"But why ever not?" Peter persisted. "You think that the returning of the Koran is a worthwhile gesture, why not the sword?"

Edward looked into Peter's face and then spoke slowly. "By reading your travel books you have at least tried to seek some of the wonders of this fascinating continent but you haven't even scratched the surface of the knowledge required to understand it. I couldn't explain to you why you are wrong in less than one year of living, sleeping and eating with its peoples."

He paused then said, "I must go now. Walk back towards the anvil and speak to the sentry for a few minutes."

"How can I contact you if I want to?"

"Send your man to Yakim Bey's tinware shop, I often go there; but there's a big battle coming soon against Ayub Khan, that will take all your time and energies."

"But how about returning the sword?"

"Forget all about it, Peter. Now, talk to the sentry. Goodbye."

"Goodbye, Edward."

After his meeting with Edward, Peter returned to his tent feeling deflated. He sat on his bed and considered the problem as he saw it. There was an equation in his mind that seemed to have a completely logical conclusion. The sword was still very influential and important to the Mujaheddin; this was obvious at the ambush when the warriors had retreated after seeing it in enemy hands. They would almost certainly band together to obtain the sword, and when they were united the British forces would have to break them into their separate parts again. So if the sword were returned the tribes would not have a reason to unite, and the British army would have no reason to fight them. Diplomacy then has a chance. Q.E.D.

Gradually he convinced himself of the wisdom of this line of argument; the battle scenes that he had witnessed recently made him eager to save any further bloodshed on either side – Afghan or British. He kept telling himself that, as the theory was sound for the jewelled Koran, so the taking of the sword from Talafi must have accentuated the problem, therefore its return could certainly subdue some of the religious fervour; it would be the opening gift.

Turning these suppositions over in his mind he realised that, right or wrong, he had to talk to Assan. If he were wrong then Assan would emphasise and corroborate Edward's point of view but if the driver agreed, he was the only person who would be able to make the first contact with the tribesmen. Finally he made the decision to talk to Assan. He picked up the jewelled tulwar that was wrapped in a field blanket, pushed aside the flap of his tent and walked out, putting on his helmet.

He made his way over to the muleteers' quarters and saw that a number of them were squatting on their haunches around a fire. As he approached the ring of firelight, a figure jumped up and trotted over to him. "You are wanting me, Sahib?"

"Yes, Assan, how did you know?"

"Oh, Sahib, you wouldn't come out here to talk to these muleteers, it must be important and so you want a driver."

"Assan, come over here by the baggage stack, away from the fire."

There, in the dim moonlight and some rays from the glowing lantern, Peter uncovered the sword and showed it to the driver. "Do you know what this is or whom it belongs to?" he asked.

Assan looked carefully at the blade with its Arabic writings and then at the jewel-studded handle. "No, Sahib, I don't know whom this beautiful tulwar belongs to. I cannot read the signs on the blade but I think these are the signs of Islam. It's certainly a most fine sword that must have belonged to someone of great importance."

"I took it from a warrior when we rescued the English lady," Peter explained. "I think that the Afghans think it has religious origins."

"Oh my goodness, then they'll come to get it back, Sahib. You must hide it very carefully otherwise they'll kill you and steal it." Assan was nervously excited.

Peter looked at the craft-worked blade and said, "I think it should be given back to the Afghans."

Assan's head bobbed up in surprise. "Oh, Sahib, why do you want to give back such a beautiful sword?"

"Because it might stop the fighting." Peter again examined the blade he held horizontally in his hands. "If it is a religious symbol, and it can be returned, then we might be able to talk to the Afghan chiefs about peace."

"You are very trusting, Sahib."

"Am I? I think its return to their religious leaders could lead to saving of many Afghan and British lives, but how could it be returned? Do any of the Mullahs in the mosques know who to contact with the Afghans?"

"Oh, Sahib, it'd be very difficult and very dangerous." Assan was wringing his hands as he spoke.

"I suppose that's right, Assan, but I've seen too many of my men die to want to go on slaughtering these tribesmen."

Assan could see that if anyone was going to be used as the contact it would have to be him. The idea terrified him to his very soul but the feeling that he would be acting bravely for the Regiment pushed him on.

"Could you find a contact I could just talk to?" Peter asked. "Will you see if you can arrange a meeting with one of their chiefs where I can hand over the tulwar with just a word of friendship. I'm sure it is worth a try."

Assan stood silently as he thought, then he said, "I have spoken to a Mujaheddin in Deh-I-Khoja. He's now old and was wounded in the last war with the British but he has a coffee shop in the town. I'll talk to him, Sahib, and try to make a meeting for you."

"Assan, I appreciate the risk you're taking but if you can manage it then the whole Regiment will be forever in your debt."

"I think you're too generous, Sahib, for it'll be only a little thing I'll do."

Peter wrapped the blade into the blanket and then said. "Assan, you just tell me where I'm to meet your contact, and I'll be there."

Chapter 16

Assan was worried. The young Sahib was obviously wanting help and while he was certain that the return of the sword might well avert more conflict, Assan was not so sure. But nevertheless his loyalty to the British and the Royal regiment pushed him to a point beyond normal reasoning. Though fully aware of the danger in his mission, his enthusiasm blinded him to the difference between the 'only just achievable' and the 'totally impossible'.

Rutland Sahib had told him that all gunners, especially of 6/8 Battery, would give him all the help they could. Though what assistance they could give him, he could not see but the idea that his action might save many British lives and earn their undying thanks, warmed his innermost soul. Nevertheless, he was still worried. He was certain that he could make contact with the local natives and even one of their leaders but whether he could convince them of the benefits of re-obtaining the sword, he was not so sure. In the centre of Deh-I-Khoja, at the lesser Hakin bazaar he stopped at a coffee house where he had previously seen the Mujaheddin.

"As-salam." He placed his palms together in greeting, and slightly bowed.

"As-salam alaikum," the owner responded.

Assan opened the conversation with the usual trivia then slowly enlarged and enriched the content until the time came for him to ask the question whether he could be taken to see one of their great and illustrious leaders. The answer was an almost definite yes, while the 'when' was only lightly touched on, and the 'where' was not mentioned.

He was offered the hospitality of a small room at the back of the shop where he was served coffee and plates of sugared sweetmeats. A newly-filled hookah was offered for him to smoke but this he refused; the inhaling of tobacco smoke through rose-scented water made him feel sick.

Eventually he was told that a great leader would see him, and that a visit would be arranged very soon.

The time spent waiting hung heavily but at last two men entered the room; one of them was carrying a hooded cloak that they instructed Assan to wear. As soon as he had donned the voluminous garment, his arms were seized and his hands bound in front of him. A small light-brown sack was pulled over his head; this was in turn covered by the large hood from the cloak. He was now blind, and a prisoner.

His guards, firmly holding his upper arms, led him out of the shop where his ears told him they were walking through the Hakim bazaar. Soon the clamour of trade died away and he could feel that they were walking up an incline and over a rutted surface. Eventually the trio stopped and Assan heard one of the guards knock on a door that, when answered, creaked open.

He was led into the dwelling, and made to sit down on the floor. The hood was pulled back, the sack removed from his head, and he was then left alone in a small empty room. Assan was frightened. He had come as a messenger from the British to the Afghans, why had they tied his hands? The blindfold was an obvious precaution but the ropes were unnecessary.

The waiting, which seemed interminable, probably only lasted an hour but it felt like a lifetime, or at least a prelude to death time.

He jerked his head up when the door opened and the guards returned. One spoke to him. "Rise."

Awkwardly he scrambled to his feet, his hands were untied and he was led out of the room and into a small courtyard that was aglare with the hot afternoon sunlight. In the centre of this area was a well, complete with lifting wheel, beside was a pomegranate tree covered with its sweetly-scented blooms and dark shiny leaves. The guards led him to an ornate door on the far side of the yard. One guard knocked and opened the door, then gestured for Assan to enter.

The interior was dimly lit and cool, the shuttered sunlight gently reflected off the white walls to illuminate the few pieces of furniture and the three-seated occupants. These three men sat at the far end of the room on large raised embroidered cushions. The central figure was a big man – very imposing in stature and countenance. A vivid new scar spread across his left temple. Assan assumed that this was the great leader, the other two presumably his lieutenants.

Assan, with clasped hands, made obeisance to the big man who did not respond by movement or gesture but simply said. "A thousand blessings of Allah the Merciful be upon you."

This religious statement cheered Assan.

"You have brought a message from the Angrezi?" the big man asked in a deep rich voice.

"Yes, Huzoor. I've been told to offer you an item that you would give much to repossess."

"Do not play with me, little one. You speak of a sword. What does the Angrezi soldier want in exchange?"

"Nothing but peace, Huzoor. He'll return the sword to you if you'll ask the Amir to use peaceful means to settle the disagreements between the Angrezi and his Excellency."

"Little one, do you wear an amulet or good luck charm around your neck?" Assan was taken aback by the question, which seemed out of context with the discussion.

"Yes, Oh Mighty One, I do."

"And when you are in need of extra courage, or luck, do you hold it in your hand to sustain yourself?"

Assan swallowed nervously. "Yes, Huzoor."

Badal leaned forward and, with hardened eyes, peered closely at Assan. "And this charm is from the Angrezilog. It is nothing to do with your religion or people but a symbol of our oppressors."

Assan was terrified, his stomach knotted and griped. How did this man know that he wore an Artillery badge on a thong about his neck? "You speak the truth, Oh All Knowing One," he murmured.

Badal sat back. "The sword of which you speak has been corrupted by the hands of the infidels. It is now a worthless piece of metal, of no use to our faith or us. Your faith in your amulet is also worthless."

Badal paused then, looking intently into Assan's eyes, continued. "You do not know of what I am about to tell you and it will clear the skin from your eyes and answer the questions in your mind as to why I took the name of 'Revenge'. The father of your master, Rutlandi, murdered my father when I was a boy and took a precious Holy Relic. This foul deed can only be revenged in blood, his blood, and it must be shed by me." Assan's bowels were in a twisted agony; their tortured flesh screamed at him as he realised the terrible position that he was in.

Badal paused, then after some thought continued. "I will send you back as a message to the Angrezi army."

Assan could have jumped with joy. This great man would not squash a small bird who had only brought a message, he would use the same small bird to take a message back to Rutland Sahib.

"To show the infidels that there is no help to be found in putting faith in holding amulets in your hand – I shall return your hand with the charm held tightly in it. And to show that I have no use for the sword I will return your head but keep your body here to feed the dogs."

Assan blanched. "But, Huzoor, I'm only a messenger. I'm not an Angrezi."

Badal raised his hand. "You are poisoned by them. You have chosen your end. You've forsaken your race and your religion. As you are divided in life so I will divide you in death." He gestured to the guards to remove the driver.

Assan shrugged off their hands. "One last word I beg, Huzoor." Badal nodded, and waved the guards to stand back. Holding himself erect Assan looked the chieftain in the eye.

"I am a true Muslim. I am a Sunni and I respect and honour the Hadith and the Koran. I will never betray my faith. I serve the British because they have an understanding of life, honour and respect even for their enemies, all greater than you natives. You have a knife at my throat but," feeling the anger in his chest, he glared at Badal "be assured that after I die they will have their 'Badal'."

The chieftain returned the glare in Assan's eyes, then he spoke gently and sincerely, "Bravely spoken, you will die like a man, little one." Then to the guards he ordered. "Kill him cleanly and quickly."

Just before dawn the rifle shot woke Peter; it was the sharp crack of a Martini Henry. Jumping to his feet he grabbed his helmet and ran towards the gun's position. He could see Sergeant Hills talking to Bombardier Smith and pointing towards Kandahar, while in his hand he held a package.

"What's the commotion, Sergeant?" called Peter.

"Don't know exactly, sir. Someone threw this package into the compound and scampered off quick like. The sentry fired at 'im but I don't think 'e was hit."

Hills held out a cloth wrapped package, it was the size of a grapefruit. The light from the fast approaching dawn was bright enough to examine the object. Peter could see that it was tied with two strips of material knotted across the top.

He carried it across to Number 1 gun position, sat on an ammunition crate and placed the package on a case in front of him. He tried to undo the knots but they were too tightly tied. Sergeant Hills who was standing beside him produced a clasp knife and promptly cut the tapes.

Peter slowly unfolded the package; he had a growing feeling of trepidation. When the last corner of the cloth was lifted, his stomach knotted at the revolting sight of the contents. It was a human hand. It was Assan's right hand. Inside the slightly parted fingers he could see the large brass gunner's badge that Assan wore on a thong around his neck. Gently Peter tugged the cold fingers apart and pulled the badge out of their rigid grasp. A few inches of leather thong still remained attached to it. He stared at Assan's prize possession, the brass of the badge cold to his touch. This significant piece of metal had been given to Assan by his father who had received it from a British Gunner to whom he had given assistance on the retreat from Kabul in 1842. Now the badge was again in the hands of a British Gunner but this time it signified very bad news for its previous owner.

"Over there, Sergeant," shouted a sentry. "On that large rock."

Sergeant Farrant, shielding his eyes from the rising sun with his hand, peered at where the sentry was pointing. Hills marched over to the men and also examined the object. Peter remained sitting by the dead hand – his head bowed deep in thought.

"Excuse me, sir."

Peter looked up at Sergeant Hills.

"I think you should come and see this, sir."

"What is it, Sergeant?" It was obviously some related horror.

"It looks like Assan's 'ead on a rock."

Peter was not surprised. He stood up and walked over to the defensive position and, shading his eyes, looked out at a rock a hundred yards in front of the section's guns. On top of the rock was balanced a round object. Sergeant Hills handed the binoculars to Peter without comment. Peter focussed them on the rock and saw the ghastly sight that he had expected to see. There was the grey bloodless countenance of Assan, his rolled turbaned hat still on his head; his eyes wide open.

"Sergeant, I'm going out to get it."

"No sir! It could easily be a trap!"

"I'm going to get it and I'm going to bury it. Bring a spade." Hills snapped out orders as Peter walked back to Number 1 gun and the opened parcel that contained Assan's hand. He picked it up carefully and started to walk out of the position holding the bundle.

"Bombardier!" shouted Hills. "Six skirmishers with carbines 50 yards in front of Lieutenant Rutland. NOW! Johnson get a spade, Sergeant Farrant lay both guns to cover both sides of that rock. Send Powell out with his rifle to shoot at anything that moves up to 600 yards away."

Peter was walking slowly and steadily out towards the rock. The gunners acting as skirmishers passed him as they ran ahead stumbling across the rock-strewn sand. Sergeant Hills trailed behind Peter, with Gunner Johnson by his side carrying a spade and a rolled-up blanket.

On reaching the rock, Peter looked at the head and saw cut into the forehead the word 'BADAL'. This poor man has suffered a terrible death because of my foolish plans, he thought.

"I'll bury him, Sergeant."

"Right, sir. Johnson start digging over there."

"Sergeant! I said I will bury him! Give me the spade." Hills gestured to the gunner to pass the spade to Peter.

"Sergeant, tell my batman to bring out my other drill jacket. I'll wrap the head in it."

"I've a blanket 'ere, sir."

"Get the jacket, Sergeant." Peter pushed the awkward Army shovel into the sand and started digging the soil. After a few minutes he removed his helmet, laid it on the ground and continued digging. Though it was early morning and the sun had little heat in it, he perspired as he worked. Then slowly as the sweat gently rolled off his forehead it became mixed with his tears. Tears of grief for a good and loyal man lost. Tears for his own stupidity. Tears for the unnecessary suffering. But as he dug deeper and the sun rose, the sweat increased and tears ended.

Bee was lying on her bed almost awake when she heard the shot. She opened her eyes – a shot, someone may be hurt. She threw back the blankets and pulled on her top clothes then, picking up a medical satchel, she pushed her way out of the tent flap.

When she arrived at the Left Section gun site she could see Peter out in front and he appeared to be digging. Sergeant Hills was standing a few yards away from him. She walked up to Sergeant Farrant who was leaning on his screw gun.

"What's happened, Sergeant?"

"Ah, Miss, well…" Farrant turned to face her, he hesitated as though confused.

"Is there some trouble?" she queried.

"No, Miss." Farrant paused. "One of the drivers is killed."

"Why is Mr Rutland digging?"

The Sergeant again hesitated. "The native was one that Lieutenant Rutland sent on a special mission." He looked at his dust-covered boots. "I shouldn't say this Miss but, confidential like, Lieutenant Rutland 'as taken it awful 'ard – 'e's insistin' on burying the man's remains 'isself."

"I see. Thank you, Sergeant." She walked forward from the screw gun and, standing completely still, watched Peter as he worked the torment out of his soul.

The prickle of tears came to her eyes as she watched this young man paying with public humiliation for his own actions. She had known for some days now that she loved him but his act of penance provoked an overwhelming feeling of love and pity for him; she wanted to hold him in her arms and comfort his anguish-wracked body against her own. She let out a sob that she stifled with her hand. Oh

Peter, Peter. The scene in front of her dissolved in tears that gently rolled down her cheeks unheeded. She stood upright, her body gently shaking with her grief.

Sergeant Farrant heard the gentle sobbing, and saw her tremble. Quietly he spoke to himself. "You're not the only one wot cares for 'im Miss – we all do in our own way."

At four feet down Peter's shovel hit solid rock; an impenetrable slab. He could dig no further. He put down the shovel and walked over to the rock where he wrapped the head up into the jacket that his batman had brought out. When he had completely covered Assan's head, he lifted it up and carried it to the prepared grave. Slowly and with reverence, he placed the two bundles containing head and hand at the bottom, and then gently he poured sand over them until the hole was filled. He smoothed off the surface, and collected a number of rocks with which he built a small cairn to mark the site of the grave.

When he had placed the last rock, Peter stood up bareheaded. He wanted to say a prayer, but what words to use, and to which God? The he remembered his father's quote from a sura in the Koran.

He spoke clearly, so that even Hills could understand.

"Allah the Merciful, the Compassionate, the Forgiver, the Forgiving, the Clement, the Generous, the Affectionate, the Kind." Finally he added, "To You we commend the spirit of this man, one of your bravest sons."

Sergeant Hills walked over to the grave, picked up Peter's helmet and handed it to him. Peter took it and placed it on his head. Slowly he walked a few yards past the rock, further away from the section position, and looked out at the desolate yet majestic scene spread out before him. He looked out towards the Pushti-Rud hills where shortly the two armies of different worlds would do terrible battle.

No tears fell from his eyes now. Instead grains of steel entered his soul as he thought of the unwarranted cruelty inflicted on Assan. The thought of revenge gave him a fire in his belly that tempered the steel in his soul. One Peter Rutland had made a terrible mistake, because of which a fine man had been savagely murdered. Now a different Peter Rutland, staring at the arid wasteland, swore his own dreadful oath.

"I will find you, Badal. I will be 'Badal'." His hatred was cold and controlled. It would be steered towards the vengeance of Assan; no other lives would be put at risk – except his own.

Peter walked back to where Sergeant Hills was standing beside the grave. He faced the cairn, drew himself upright to attention and pronounced in a quiet and firm voice. "A brave man has died and lies here."

Both Officer and Sergeant came crisply to the salute. They paused for a few seconds then turned away and, one behind the other, returned to the screw guns.

Chapter 17

Peter pulled off his helmet and entered his tent. Beside his bed a canvas bucket hung on a tent pole. He unhooked it and poured water into a canvas bowl on a three-legged stand, to wash the dust and sweat of digging from his face and hands.

He pulled off his jacket and threw it onto the bed then, rolling his sleeves up, he plunged his hands into the water and threw it up onto his face and neck. It helped to clear his head. He had an idea stirring there but a little more time was needed for it to form properly.

"May I come in?"

He looked over his shoulder; the water ran off his chin and onto his shirt. Bee was standing by the tent-flap. Peter nodded and leaned over the bowl.

"Was the driver someone special?" Bee asked softly.

Peter continued to peer into the dirty water in the bowl. "Assan? Special. Yes he was. He trusted me. I asked him to do the impossible and sent him to a horrible death."

Bee stepped forwards and placed her hand on his back. "Oh, my dear, don't tear at yourself. This man did for you what you would have done for him."

"Yes." Peter looked at her. "That's exactly it. I had decided that in my own mind a few minutes ago but you've put it into words. I must go and avenge him."

"Avenge him?" her hand dropped to her side. "How?"

Peter stood upright, shook his wet hands and dried them on a towel. "I'm going into Deh-I-Khoja to find this man Badal, and I'm going to kill him."

"Badal, who is he?"

"A man who wants revenge on my family. He's tried to kill me once already, and now has killed Assan."

"But 'Badal' is Pushtu for revenge."

Peter looked at her. "I know. You look surprised. Why?"

"Because yesterday I spoke to a dhoolie carrier who told me that 'Talafi' was revenge in Dari."

"Dari. What's that?"

"It's a dialect used in the hills of Afghanistan. So maybe your Badal is Talafi, my guard and the man with the jewelled sword."

"Good God. If I'd killed him…" Peter stopped. "He's the one that Edward Anstruther has been hearing of. I must find him and kill him."

"Don't be a fool," cried Bee, "How can you find this man in amongst the Afghans? You're a British officer, remember? How can you wander through an Afghan town, kill Badal and get out again?"

"I'll go disguised as a native; Edward can disappear into a crowd – so can I. I'm the only person who knows what Badal or Talafi looks like, so only I can kill him."

Bee's emotions were in a state of turmoil. This man, who she so desperately loved, was showing no signs of affection towards her and was about to throw his life away on a futile gesture.

"You can't speak any of the languages," she said. "How're you going to find out where the man is? What if someone asks you a question?"

"I'll dress in dirty rags and act as a dumb imbecile. I can reach the tinware shop that sells cups and contact the shopkeeper, he'll act as the go between."

"Peter, you're a proud fool," Bee condemned him, her eyes filling with tears of frustration. "You lose the life of a brave man through a mistake, then prepare to waste your own. You'll even risk the lives of your own men just for your pompous attitude towards honour."

Peter hung his head as he weighed her words. Was he overreacting to Assan's death? Possibly, but he knew that Badal was an important asset for the enemy.

"I'm going," he murmured determinedly.

"Then I am coming with you."

"No you mustn't"

"Why?"

"It's too dangerous."

"I speak Pushtu. It'll be less dangerous with me leading an idiot through the town than an idiot going on his own. Remember I also know Badal or Talafi. If we succeed, many lives will be saved – if we fail, what are another two."

"You cannot come."

"Why not?"

"Because…"

"Because what?" Bee demanded.

Peter placed his hands on her arms and looking into her eyes said. "Because I love you."

"Oh, Peter." But words were not to be. They grasped each other in a desperate embrace, their lips meeting in a kiss that told each other of their overwhelming love. They clung together swaying slightly with the fervour of their affection. Eventually their lingering caresses slowed until they stood holding each other in the warmth and closeness of their encircling arms.

Pressing Bee's head against his, Peter spoke quietly to her. "You know that I must go to the town and you know you can't come. Please help me with your knowledge of the tribesmen to disguise me; I must have your help but not in the city. You understand that don't you?"

He stopped, waiting for a reply. While she listened to him, she realised his determination, and at the same time decided how to get help. She would tell Tim.

She hugged him tighter. "I don't want to lose you."

"Then help me." Standing back from Peter she looked him in the face. "Alright. I'll go and get clothing and dyes." She lightly kissed him on the lips again, smiled then pushed her way out of the tent.

Peter decided that now was the time he must write a letter to his parents. It might be his last, and there was a lot of explaining to do. He picked up his writing pad and, sitting on the edge of his bed, started to write.

Five minutes later Tim lifted the tent flap and entered. He looked very serious; in his hand he held a small leather box.

"Hello, Tim. Anything wrong?"

"I've just seen Bee, she has told me everything."

"But—"

Tim raised his hand and spoke sharply. "Listen!" He sat down on the bed beside Peter.

"She's told me of your plan, and that you are both in love. She said she doesn't want your to go but understands it might be necessary. Now tell me the full story."

Peter closed the writing pad and related the complete history from the meeting with Edward up to Assan's death. He made it a factual report knowing that Tim would understand his position regarding responsibility.

"So Assan died trying to fulfil your orders which Anstruther had said were a waste of time."

"That's it," agreed Peter.

"Your chances of finding this man Badal are so remote as to make your visit useless." Peter looked ready to press his position but Tim continued, "You could well be killed without achieving anything. The Battery can't afford to lose another officer. But," he stood up and leaned against the tent pole, "Anstruther should be told of this man and his actions. Your description of Badal could be of great importance."

Tim looked up as a figure appeared at the tent entrance. It was Bee holding a bundle of clothing and a small bag. She came in and put her hand on Peter's shoulder. "I'm sorry, Peter, but I had to tell Tim." He smiled and nodded. "I understand." He held her hand and squeezed it.

"Peter," said Tim, "I'm senior to you by a couple of months, so here are your orders. Bee will disguise you and lead you to the tinware shop. You will attempt to contact

Anstruther but if you can't meet him within three hours you will leave a written description of Badal, and a message asking Edward to meet you in the mule-lines tonight." This was a side of the usually flippant Tim that Peter had not previously seen.

"Finally, even if you do see Badal, you will NOT attempt to kill him," Tim emphasised the statement. "I'm certain you'd do more harm than good. Do you understand?" It was obvious really. Of course Tim was right.

"Yes I understand."

"Good." Tim opened the leather box he held and took out a small revolver and leather ammunition pouch. "My father bought this for me to wear on the occasions when the military revolver was too heavy. It's a .38 Webley Pryse and, I'm told, a good 'man-stopper'."

He closed the case and placed it on the bed. Peter was deeply moved by Tim's concern. He was prepared to accept the full responsibility for Peter's venture only because of his marginal superiority. "Thank you Tim – for everything. I'll do exactly as you have said but I won't be under your orders, it's my responsibility."

"We'll see about that. Now Bee get this man looking like an Afghan."

"An idiot Afghan," she added.

"Shouldn't be difficult. Now, Rutland, get undressed."

Peter stripped to his underwear and put on a belt with the revolver holster and ammunition pouch around his waist.

Bee threw a filthy nightshirt-like galabea over his head to cover him from the neck downwards. She produced a pair of worn rope and leather sandals for him to wear, and then she opened her bag and took out a bottle of iodine. A few drops of this she mixed with a little water and sponged it evenly over Peter's face, neck, hands and feet until he had an even tanned appearance. While the skin was still damp with this liquid she wiped dust onto his forehead and hair.

"God what a wreck," murmured Tim.

Finally she picked up a length of dirty material, six feet long and eighteen inches wide, that she skilfully wound around his head to form a piled turban. She was just tucking in the end when Sergeant Hills called from outside. "Lieutenant Rutland, Sir."

"Come in, Sergeant," replied Peter.

Hills ducked through the entrance, stood upright and his mouth dropped open. He looked at Tim and Bee. "I'm sorry sir, I thought I 'eard Lieutenant Rutland."

"You did," said Peter.

"Oh my Gawd," exclaimed Hills. "You're going into the town."

"That's right. I'll be back about mid afternoon. What d'you want?"

"Captain Dainby is on 'is way; 'e's with the centre section now but 'e's coming 'ere."

"Quick – outside," Tim ordered. "I'm about to throw you off the gun position. Head for the town gates. Bee can join you there shortly."

Dainby could be seen further down the defence line talking to Centre Section. He walked up towards Left Section with the Battery Sergeant Major at his side.

"Tailby. Where's Rutland?"

"Arranging the clover and grass for the battery mules, sir."

Dainby nodded. "I want you both at the Battery Office at 1500 hours."

"Very good, sir."

The Captain stood and slowly looked around the gun site. All was tidy and in order. The sentry teams were standing to attention. He was about to leave when his eye fell on Peter. "What the hell is that?"

"One of the grass-cutters, sir. He's wandered over from the mule lines; I think he's a bit stupid. I was about to kick him out."

"Well do so now!"

"Right, sir. Sergeant, push this object towards the mule lines and kick his backside. Maybe he'll remember not to come back."

Hills caught hold of Peter's shoulder and roughly pulled him towards the defensive line. Peter shuffled along his head lolling from side to side. Dainby, Tim and Bee watched as Hills pushed Peter between the guns and gave him a kick with a shout of "And don't come back."

Peter fell and sprawled out. He picked himself up and half bowed a salaam then, with a shuffling gait, set off towards the town gate of Deh-I-Khoja.

The sentry on the gate took no notice of the continuous flow of Afghans moving through as Bee led the shambling figure towards the bazaar. They walked through a stall-lined alley; past beggars and coffee shops, butchers and sewage ditches. Twice Bee stopped to ask the way to Yakim Bey's. Eventually, down a wide alley, they came to the tinware shop. A young man, dressed in a pale blue galabea, was standing in the shadow at the back of the shop. As Bee and Peter entered the man came forward brandishing a light stick and shouting. They both backed out of the entrance.

"He doesn't like women or idiots," Bee murmured. She led Peter a few yards from the shop then crouched down on her heels against a wall, pulling him down beside her.

"We'll be beggars and watch the entrance."

Time dragged by as they sat with outstretched hands. They waited for about an hour but still there was no sign of Edward. All was not wasted though, for between them they had been given three small coins.

Peter was thinking hard on what other action he could take when a man dressed in a dark blue chagri cloak threw down a coin. "Send your woman home and buy another mug made in Rutland." The man spoke softly in English. Peter managed to keep surprise from his face. He made a salaam, and with his head lolling about he watched the man walk on down the road.

"Bee. Go back to the Battery." He spoke out of the corner of his mouth.

She turned her head to face him. They looked into each other's eyes. A thousand thoughts sped between them but not a word was spoken. Bee knew she had to leave but she was very worried. Peter stopped his head lolling for a second – and smiled. Bee got up and, without comment or gesture, walked back the way they had come.

Peter waited a few minutes until there was no one at or near the shop, and then clumsily he rose and shuffled across to the shop entrance. The young man, seeing his approach, walked into the back of the shop and stood in the shadows holding back a bead curtain. Peter followed him into the gloom.

"Stay here," was the whispered instruction. He stood motionless in the dim light and waited. "Follow me." A door was held ajar. Peter stepped through and there, seated on a rug by a small table, was the man in the blue chagri cloak.

"Well done, Peter," he said, "You certainly fooled me. But next time you're a beggar, remember never to offer your left hand."

"Edward! Am I pleased to see you!"

"I presume it is me you want to see?"

"Yes. I've some information that I think'll be of use to you." Peter related all that had happened since their last meeting, including Assan's death.

When he had finished, Edward looked at him. "You're a young man who has learned a lot about this life in a very short time. Don't be hard on yourself for your mistake with Assan. Now describe this man Badal or Talafi."

"He is six feet tall, broad build, black hair, booming voice and almost certainly a vivid scar on his temple."

"Aha, or a bandage! I know the man; he's a senior chief. So he is the uniter of the tribes is he?" The young man from the front of the shop came into the room. Edward spoke to him in Pushtu, giving instructions.

"I've arranged for you to go back to the lines in a load of alfalfa feed. Mustafa is organising it," Edward explained. "You might've felt tempted to try and kill this Badal but now we know who he is we can follow and watch him, that is much better than having a corpse." Peter nodded his understanding, fully aware of how close his hot-headedness had nearly brought him to a second bad mistake.

"I must get this information out at once," continued Edward. "It is of the utmost importance. I have proved that your jewelled Koran is of enormous religious and political value and I am confident that I can contact the correct religious authority. But should it fall into the hands of Badal it would be ruinous for Afghanistan. This man would use it entirely for his own advancement and not for the religion of the people."

He leaned back against the pile of cushions on the floor. "I am certain that its return to the correct hands will greatly assist the stabilisation of the country but it must not be offered as if it was handed over by the military. It must be returned in the correct and diplomatic fashion. There is to be a large battle tomorrow, you must take the Koran with you – do not leave it in your camp. Nowhere is it safe other than secretly with you."

He looked over his shoulder at a door leading into the back storeroom. "Where is Mustafa? He should have found the cart by now." He got up from the carpet, opened the back door and stepped through. After a few moments he returned and waved Peter to follow him. Outside in the little courtyard, an old man was squatting down holding the lead rope of a donkey, which was attached to a small cart laden with green stalks of alfalfa.

Edward pulled off two large armsful. "Get in. I'll cover you up," he ordered. Peter clambered onto the rickety cart.

"Goodbye, Edward." A pile of sweet smelling greenery swamped over him, and a few minutes later he felt the cart move out into the back alleyway.

Having seen the cart well clear of the back of the shop, Edward returned to the room. He was puzzled that Mustafa had not come back to tell him that the cart was ready. He picked up a small cup of thick treacly Turkish coffee from the side table and, still standing, he drained it to the dregs.

With a crash the door at the front burst open. A tall bearded figure sprang across the room and pushed a thin bladed knife against Edward's throat. He stayed motionless; he knew that one false move and the needle tip would pierce his windpipe. Another man entered the room dragging a body behind him. The corpse was Mustafa; his throat had been cut from ear to ear.

Lastly a large man entered. Edward instantly knew it was Badal. It all added up – the face, the build and the low-bandaged turban.

"So you speak English." Badal smiled. "I also speak it."

Edward remained silent. "But why do you speak English to a beggar? Maybe the beggar was English – but you would only mention Rutland if the beggar was that man." Edward cursed his own stupidity for saying that unnecessary word to Peter.

"Where is he now?" Edward said nothing. So Mustafa had not betrayed them nor had he talked. Badal does not yet know yet where Peter is. I will have to tell them eventually as they torture me but by that time Peter will be safe.

"Search the other rooms," Badal instructed the other man.

Within a few minutes the small building had been completely ransacked and nothing found.

"You feel content that Rutland has now escaped." Badal smiled. "But it doesn't matter. I will kill him in tomorrow's battle. I know where his little guns will be." He nodded at the guard. "Kill him."

The thin blade cut the skin, then the windpipe and finally it pierced the jugular vein. Edward crumpled and slumped to the floor. With the last of his draining consciousness, he saw an English garden on a summer's day – a young woman dressed in white was coming towards him, her arms outstretched.

Chapter 18

Badal smiled as, from his high vantage point, he watched the British infantry moving into its battle formation below him. Through his binoculars he could see the two screw guns moving over towards the left of the soldiers with the bare knees. He gave a deep chuckle.

Soon those little guns will be mine, and I will feel Rutland's blood flowing across my hands. I shall slaughter him like a sheep; a throat slashed to the spine bleeds the body well.

The morning heat bounced in shining waves off the surrounding rocks as he rose from his hidden viewpoint, and moved down towards his large group of followers.

Badal stopped in his descent of the slope and looked at the gathering. These men will die for me; Rutland will die slowly by my hand, and I will rejoice. The satisfaction at the imminent achievement of revenge inwardly cheered him. He laughed again – a short booming laugh.

The dawn start for the Field Force meant that all sections of infantry, cavalry and artillery had covered most of the distance marching to their respective start-lines before the sun had reached its full strength. Even so Peter was pleased when a halt was called while the infantry reorganised into their attack formations. His men had learned, during the march from Kabul, to be cautious in the use of their water bottles. They knew how much worse was a savage afternoon thirst when their canteens were dry, than the normal morning thirst when water was available. They were prepared to suffer the discomfort of the earlier to reduce the torment of the latter.

The mules were amazing. Cavalry horses suffered terribly in the excessive heat and arid atmosphere but the pack animals just calmly conserved moisture and energy. They always drank deeply when offered a mountain stream but rarely showed signs of distress when thirsty.

While Left Section waited for its orders, the gunners sat or lay down to rest. It never ceased to amaze Peter that the men could sleep for the shortest period, in the worst conditions, at any time; even after a good night's rest.

Captain Dainby strode over to the section and addressed Peter in a loud voice. "Rutland. Get these men on their feet at once, they look like idle layabouts."

"Certainly, sir," Peter replied but did nothing to actually comply with the instructions. "You have positional orders for me, sir?" he queried.

Dainby drew a plan out of his map wallet and laid out the partially folded sheet on the packs of an ammunition mule. "We're here. The Gordon Highlanders will move across that open area. You're to position yourself on the north-east face of that hill. From there you'll be able to command a view in front of the Highlanders' attack. Understand?"

"Yes, sir. Is the hill cleared of tribesmen?"

"Of course it is. Any more damn fool questions?"

"What Regiment is on it? I don't want to tangle with any of our men."

"Rutland. If you can't tell the difference between a British soldier and an Afghan in his nightshirt, then I suggest you resign your commission," Dainby snapped. "Now stop shirking and get your men moving, and remember I do not want any of my orders questioned in any way today."

Peter's anger boiled up. "Of course, sir. If I can understand them." He saluted and turned to Sergeant Hills who, on seeing Dainby's choler, had quietly roused all the men to stand by their posts.

"Sergeant. Left Section. File ahead. March." In silent fury Peter strode to the head of the section. Dainby's insinuations, where his men could overhear them, were intolerable.

We are being sent off without a map, to a hill that is supposed to be cleared and might or might not be occupied by British soldiers. What a mess!

Peter, still walking, turned and called out, "Sergeant Hills. Here if you please." He faced the front and looked for the hill that was their objective. He could see the Gordons over to his right; they were in column of march but obviously at rest.

"You want me, sir?"

"Yes, Sergeant. We've been ordered to climb that hill over there," he pointed to the right front, "and position ourselves on the north east face where we'll have a clear field of fire to support the Highlanders. They'll be attacking across that open ground with their objective presumably being that far range of hills." While Peter explained the details to Hills he realised that he must contact the Gordons to find out the path of their advance, the object of their attack and the time of their start.

"Is the 'ill clear though, sir?"

"That, Sergeant, I do not know. Captain Dainby says it is but he doesn't know who cleared it or if they're still there."

"Then maybe we should advance with a skirmish line ahead of us, sir." Of course that was the answer. Trust Hills to think of that. Good old steady Hills. Peter looked at him and smiled.

"You're absolutely right, Sergeant. Thank goodness you've got a cool head on your shoulders. I expect even I would've thought of that eventually." Hills gave a small smile. He was on the point of turning away to give the necessary orders when Peter stopped him by placing a hand on his arm.

"Hills," he paused, searching for the right words. "I've never felt lonely in this command. Your experience has been a godsend to me. When we've fought this battle, I'm going to see Major Tenet to press for your promotion to Warrant Officer."

The Sergeant was completely taken by surprise. No officer had ever spoken to him in this way – like an equal. He had grown to like this young man; in fact grown fond of him in an almost brotherly fashion. But he never expected thanks for what was after all only his duty.

"Thank you very much, sir," he mumbled.

Peter then gave his instructions. "Keep the section moving towards the hill. I'm going over to that company of the Gordons to find out their plan of action. I should catch you up in about a mile. Do not go up the slope until I arrive."

"Very good, sir."

By the time Peter had run over to the Highlanders' position, found out their attack details, and returned to the screw guns, they were already at the foot of the slope leading up the hill. He could see Hills had put a skirmish line of six men ahead of the section, and that all the gunners and drivers were holding their carbines ready to use. Peter ran past the line of mules up to Sergeant Hills who was standing at the head of the section. He paused for a few seconds to recover his breath, then quickly told Hills of the Highlanders' plan of action.

"We've about an hour to find a good fire base and get into action. Plenty of time without the enemy but not a lot with them."

"Shall I send the skirmishers on, sir?"

"Yes please, Sergeant. We'll move directly up the hill heading just to the left of the crown so we can swing round to cover the advance. That right-hand side looks much too steep for comfort."

Hills gave orders to the six skirmishers that sent them scrambling off up the slope. The section followed in two columns; one for each gun. The hillside was covered with small rocks and boulders but none was large enough to hide a man. After thirty minutes the skirmishers reached the crest and started to swing around the left shoulder. Thank goodness there were no signs of any enemy tribesmen having been there.

At the crest Peter found a good fire platform for both guns on the north-east face where they could command the rocky ridge beyond which he could not see. He was surprised to see that on his left front there was a valley with moderately steep sides eventually lifting up to a craggy hill almost in front of him.

"Sergeant, use that area over there." He pointed to the flat scree close to where he was standing. "Action front."

"Action Front!" The gunners and mules acted by reflex so that three minutes later two mountain pieces were ready for use; ammunition to the front and mules to the rear. Peter meanwhile had been scanning the ground over which the infantry were to advance, and also the rocky ridge that was their objective. He could see no sign of any tribesmen, though some of the rock clusters might have been sangars and could have small groups of men hidden in them. The part that looked the most defensible was the craggy hill on the opposite side of the valley below him. A footpath appeared to run diagonally from the low left in the valley up to the high right on the far edge. There were plenty of places for groups of men to hide unseen in those boulders but they would not be able to fire at the advancing infantry.

Then from high up on the gun site the gunners could hear a piper playing the Highlanders into the attack, the swirling music drifted high onto the hill. The Gordons were advancing in an extended line spread across half a mile of the plain. Their rifles, with bayonets fixed, were held at the high port.

Beyond the advancing Highlanders, at least one company of Ghurkhas could be seen. Their Martini Henrys also at the high port as they advanced step for step with the Gordons. The two regiments of the world's finest soldiers moved at a steady pace up the slope, which seemed to be clear of any tribesmen.

Just short of the skyline, the infantry stopped. Some officers, crouching low, moved to the topmost edge and peered over. They could be seen slowly relaxing as they found that there was no sign of the enemy – at least in the immediate vicinity beyond the ridge.

Peter was just wondering what to do next, whether to stay in action awaiting orders or to limber up ready for a move, when he heard the clatter of a horse's hooves on the stony ground. To his amazement it was Captain Dainby riding up the hill towards their position. He spurred his mount right up to Number 1 gun's position and called "Rutland. I want this gun moved. Have it limber up."

"Very good sir. Sergeant Hills, Number 1 gun limber up." He was surprised at the unusual order. Was his section to be split up?

"Where do you want me to take the gun, sir?"

"You'll remain here Rutland. I want this gun under your Sergeant to drop down to the valley and climb that hill on your left front. They'll be able to cover the Highlanders' advance with a wider field of fire." Using his glasses Peter examined the rocky hill that Dainby had identified.

"Has the hill been taken, sir?" There was plenty of cover for the enemy to easily ambush anyone on the track.

"Of course it has. Don't prevaricate. Get your sluggards moving."

Peter glared at the Captain. Dainby was often uncaring and intolerant but never so blatantly callous. He appeared to be nervous; his horse was continuously nodding its head and moving its hooves. Dainby was twitching the reins in his hands, pulling his horse's mouth about and causing it to be restless. There was something strange about the whole scene. Dainby was acting in a most unusual way; there was something wrong about his appearance. Peter could not put his finger on the point of query but he decided to be firm.

"I'll leave Sergeant Hills here, sir, and go myself with Number 1 gun."

Dainby's face became puce with fury. He kicked his horse forward so that its chest almost knocked into Peter. He leaned over to speak loudly and directly into Peter's face.

"You will do as you are ordered and you will do it now. Send your gun out this instant."

Sergeant Hills, who had witnessed this incredible outburst, marched over to Peter saluted and said, "Number 1 gun ready to move, sir."

"Right, Sergeant. As you climb up that track have skirmishers out, and all men are to carry carbines. I can give you covering fire if you come under—"

"Oh for God's sake, Rutland. Get this gun moving and stop your dithering," exploded Dainby. Peter ignored this tirade. "Sergeant, if you come under attack you will retire—"

"He will do no such thing unless I order it," Dainby interrupted. "Do you hear, Sergeant? You're under my direct orders now. Move your men down that track at once."

"Yes, sir." Hills turned and called out to his crew, "Number 1 gun forward march."

As the mules moved off, Hills started to organise his men for scouting and prepare them against any surprise ambush.

"What do you want us to do, sir?" Peter asked the Captain.

"You're to remain here to support the infantry until I want you. You are not to move, do you understand?"

"Yes, sir," replied Peter but he did not understand why his Number 2 gun should remain in such a useless position when his Number 1 gun was moving forward to a better field of fire but out of his control, and into a possible danger area. Dainby tugged viciously on the reins pulling his horse's head round to descend the slope; within a few minutes he had disappeared from sight.

Peter watched Sergeant Hills' gunners descending the steep track down the valley. He must be ready to assist them if any danger was seen, however small. "Sergeant Farrant." he called, "Keep a careful watch on the track up that rocky hill ahead. If there's any sign of movement let me know at once."

"Yessir." Farrant instructed his gunners to also keep scanning the rocks ahead.

Peter then thought of Powell's incredible long-distance eyesight. "Gunner Powell, come here."

Powell ran over to him. "Sir?"

"You're to watch the area above the track on that far hill for any movement. Be ready to shoot. You've got your rifle I hope?" Peter smiled.

"Never without it, sir. I was surprised to see Captain Dainby with a carbine though, sir. He had it in a boot on his saddle."

That was it! That was what looked wrong. Dainby was sitting on an NCO's saddle with a carbine in the boot. Why? It was his usual horse but it was not his own saddle. Maybe his had been damaged, or even lost but why carry a carbine? There was something amiss. It was all too strange.

"Sergeant Farrant. Load Number 2 gun. Common shell."

Farrant showed his surprise. "Load with common shell, sir?"

"Yes."

"Very good, sir." Something inside was telling Peter there was trouble ahead. He peered down at Sergeant Hills who had already reached the valley and was crossing over the rough dried-up riverbed. His gunners, holding their carbines, were walking either side of the line of mules, continuously looking around.

"Lieutenant Rutland, sir," Farrant called out. "There's an 'ighlander coming up the slope on our right."

"Thank you, Sergeant." Peter looked down to see a kilted figure clambering up the rock shale side of the gun position. Through the binoculars it looked as though the approaching figure was Lieutenant Angus Hamilton. Peter returned to inspecting the track up which Hills was now moving.

"We meet again," a Scottish voice broke Peter's concentration.

"Hello, Angus. Yes we meet again. What made you climb all the way up here?"

"Well, Peter, my CO has been trying to contact your Battery Commander but without success. Major MacDonald wanted to explain the area we're moving into, and has asked for your support."

Peter looked at Angus and thought, this is the same request your brother made on my first action; he is now dead. "I'm afraid I don't know where our BC, Captain Dainby, is. Have you details you could leave with me for when I see him?"

"Certainly." Out of his tunic pocket Angus pulled a sheet of paper. It was a pencil sketch map of the immediate surroundings showing the position of Peter's gun, the rocky hill that Sergeant Hills was climbing and the land beyond the ridge that the Highlanders at present occupied.

"We're going to advance straight over the ridge and swing round to the left sharply. There are enemy positions ahead defending the villages of Pir Pamal and Kharoti. Major MacDonald would like your guns down there at the mouth of the valley to sweep the ground in front of us. Your centre section is covering the Ghurkha company. Can that be done?"

"Yes certainly. I'll inform Captain Dainby as soon as I see him. At present he has instructed my Number 1 gun to move up the hill over there to cover your advance. They'll certainly be able to range right into the village." The situation seemed more sensible to Peter now. Obviously Dainby had known of the Infantry's intentions and had positioned Number 1 gun well in advance.

"I think Captain Dainby'll return here shortly to move me down into the valley. If he doesn't arrive within twenty minutes, I'll move regardless and come into action where you require me in the valley."

"Thank you, Peter, I'll report to the Major. Join me in a drink after the action." Peter inwardly flinched at this repeat of a gesture of hospitality that so sadly went astray last time with Angus's brother. "Yes, Angus, I'll be pleased to. Thank you. We'll certainly work up a thirst."

The Highlander turned away and started to scramble down the steep track to return to his company. "Angus," Peter cupped his hands and called out, "Take care."

The kilted officer stopped in his descent to look up at the gunner; he smiled and waved in acknowledgement. Peter watched him right to the very bottom of the slope. "Take great care, Angus," he murmured to himself.

Chapter 19

"I can see a leg in them rocks, sir!" It was Gunner Powell who had called out.

"Where?" Peter snatched up the field glasses. "Where, Powell?"

"Almost on the far edge of the hill, sir. Just above the track. Two hundred yards ahead of the skirmishers."

Peter focussed on the hill – and saw it. A leg half covered with white cloth. It must be an ambush.

"Number 2 gun 1000 yards. Can you see the aiming point? Farrant?"

"Yessir."

"Fire." Farrant heaved the gun spike over and sighted the gun, which was already loaded with common shell, onto the tumble of rocks. Quickly he stepped back and called, "Fire!"

The Number 5 jerked the lanyard; the little gun barked out its warning to the potential ambushers, and to the gunners of Number 1 gun. The shell struck too high up on the rocks but it had the required effect. The gunners could see tribesmen moving along the hill just above the track.

"2 rounds Shrapnel 900 yards. Fire," ordered Peter. He moved his binoculars onto the line of mules and gunners below. Sergeant Hills had stopped the section; the men were kneeling with their carbines at the ready. Peter ran to the edge of his gun position and slowly waved his arm in a wide sweep, indicating to Hills to retire down the valley.

Number 2 gun banged out again, the smoke obliterated Peter's view. He ran upwind to the other side of the gun site and again waved to Hills who was already turning the mules around on the narrow track. His skirmishers were falling back in readiness to act as a rear guard for the retiring gun.

Peter watched Hills run down to the lower mules and set them off down towards the valley then scramble back, carbine in hand, towards the rear guard. The tribesmen hidden in ambush were no longer visible but Peter decided to pepper the area just in case they intended to charge down the track onto the retiring screw gunners.

"2 rounds Shrapnel. Fire." He had just shouted the order when he saw the mule, second from the bottom, fall down and lie kicking on the track. An Afghan sniper lying just above the track had shot it, and the dying animal was now holding up the complete line of gunners.

"Powell," Peter yelled. "Here with your rifle."

The Afghan was in a cluster of rocks on top of a large sloping rock. As Powell arrived, Peter pointed across the valley. "There's an Afghan in those rocks near the track just above that big slab."

"I can see him, sir." Powell lay down and adjusted his sights to 900 yards. "Will you watch for the splash of my shot, sir, so I can alter for the wind."

"Alright," snapped Peter. The tribesman was not wearing white or black as they normally did, he appeared to be wearing a light brown coat. He fired again at the line of gunners trapped on the narrow track and another mule fell to its knees.

Powell rested his rifle on a rock, steadied himself, held his breath and fired. Peter saw a splash of silver as the bullet struck the smooth face of the large rock. "You're thirty feet under him and three feet to the left," he called.

While Powell reloaded and adjusted his sights, Peter saw the tribesman lean over the rock to get a better aim at the mules and gunners below, who still did not know where the shots were coming from.

Crack! Powell's rifle ripped another bullet into the air across the valley. "Six feet under him and dead in line."

This time the Afghan had seen the splash of the bullet or maybe had even been hit by pieces of rock splattering around him for he looked up to see where the shot came from. It was then that Peter could see through his binoculars that the sniper was not a tribesman. It was Captain Dainby!

He must be mad! He was shooting at his own men and had killed two mules. Dainby now leaned out even more to shoot yet again at the gunners. His shoulders and back were clearly visible as he hung over the rock.

It was in that precarious position that Powell's bullet slammed into his spine. His head jerked upwards as he arched his back at the fatal blow. First his carbine fell from his hands and clattered down the rock to fall on the mules below, then Dainby's body followed a few seconds later; the blood from his massive chest-wound leaving a long, dark smear across the smooth slab rock face as he slid down its surface.

Peter watched Hills run over to the fallen officer lying on the track, and bend over him. The gunners were heaving the dead gun mules over the edge to clear the path. Dainby's body was then laid on the back of an ammunition mule. Hills' gun crew again started on their tortuous journey back towards the valley floor; this time they were unmolested by sniper fire or tribesmen.

"Sergeant Farrant. Number 2 gun Limber up. Send a messenger down to Sergeant Hills to tell him to wait in the valley where we'll meet him."

"Very good, sir."

While the crew limbered up the screw gun, Peter stood thinking about Dainby. It looked as though he had pushed Number 1 gun into an ambush and, for some reason, had even assisted the enemy by shooting at his own men. It was impossible but it seemed to be the only answer.

"Number 2 gun ready to move, sir," reported Farrant.

"Lead on down the track, Sergeant," replied Peter.

Down in the now roasting heat of the valley the two gun crews joined together to become a full section again.

Sergeant Hills walked over to Peter together with a driver who was leading a mule carrying Dainby's body; an ammunition cover draped over it. Peter pulled back the tarpaulin sheet to see that the heavy bullet had struck the Captain in the centre of his back; he had leaned over just far enough to give Powell a good aiming point.

He replaced the canvas and said, "Ensure that Captain Dainby's body is kept covered until we have returned to Kandahar."

"Very good, sir," replied Hills and instructed the driver to take the mule back to the moving line of guns. When the man was out of earshot, Hills turned to Peter and said, "Captain Dainby was still alive when I reached 'im, sir."

"Was he indeed? That's very surprising after that fall."

"'E appeared to slide down the rock face and only fell the last ten feet onto the track." Hills paused then continued slowly, "'E said something strange to me though, sir."

"He was able to speak to you with that wound in his chest? What did he say?" Peter asked.

"'E 'ad fallen onto 'is side so I sat 'im against the rock face. 'Is eyes was open and 'e seemed conscious. I asked what 'ad 'appened. At first 'e just choked, 'alf laughed and then said. 'Nothing. Nothing 'appened.' I tried to undo 'is jacket to see 'ow bad 'e was but 'e pushed me off, 'is eyes were tight shut with the pain and then 'e laughed again, with a choke 'e said, 'I only wanted one screw gun – for me old age.' I 'eard it clear so I didn't get it wrong, that's exactly what 'e said, sir. But I don't understand what 'e meant."

So that was it, Dainby had arranged with the Afghans to deliver a mountain gun into their hands for gold; enough to retire on. "No, Sergeant. I don't understand either," Peter replied. They strode on for a while then he asked, "What are your losses?"

"We lost three carrying mules but've managed to recover the ammo. Gunners 'inks and Griffin are wounded but can walk — but the strange thing is Gunner 'amblin 'as disappeared."

"Disappeared! What do you mean?" Peter knew Hamblin well, he was the son of a small farmer in Somerset; a reliable man of great strength and large frame. A most unlikely person to go absent.

"Well sir 'e'd 'elped me with Captain Dainby and I told 'im to tie the Captain's body on to a mule. 'amblin said that 'cause the Captain fell down the cliff from above us, 'e must have ridden 'is 'orse up above on another track. Shortly after that 'e disappeared. I've an 'orrible feeling he's gone to find the Captain's 'orse."

"Damn fool!" Peter exploded. "If he runs into any Afghans I only hope he dies quickly. We can't look for him now, we've got to position ourselves further on near the valley entrance to support the infantry." Peter looked at his watch. "They'll be starting their attack in thirty-five minutes. Rejoin your gun, Sergeant."

Hills saluted and ran off up the moving Section to put himself at the head of his gun crew. Peter walked beside the line of laden mules. The 'jinkety jink' of the equipment was a perpetual background noise to his thoughts.

It took fifteen minutes of sharp marching to leave the valley, and pass clear of the rocky hill where the ambush had been set. The opposite slope down from the Highlanders' ridge could be seen to be slightly steeper than the incline up. The infantry would have quite a slide as they came down.

Peter viewed the forward area and noticed, one and a half miles away, a cluster of mud-brick buildings ringed with stone-walled fields and orchards. Presumably that was the village of Pir Pamal; Kharoti must be further over the ridge, and out of sight. He could see numerous rock sangars in front of the village with many of them clustered about with tribesmen who were dressed in their white baggy robes.

Large black or multicoloured banners were flying from poles stuck into small piles of rocks beside the sangars.

Scanning the area carefully through his glasses, he could not see any sign of enemy artillery but the Afghan pieces could easily be hidden by rock gun emplacements and so not visible from this position, which was low.

"Sergeant Hills," Peter pointed to a level area that was ideal for a gun site. "Action front over there." Hills and Farrant repeated the orders and swiftly the two screw guns were assembled with ready ammunition stacked close behind.

Now that the general view of the forward area had settled into Peter's mind, he started looking for specific details. The sangars near the village were obvious, then he spotted that a dozen or more were scattered in tumbled rock starting about 1000 yards away. To the left of the gun position was a depression, which could well be the entrance to a large nullah. It was unlikely that any Afghans were in the dried-up watercourse because, though hidden now, they could easily be cut off later on but better be careful he thought.

"Left section Number 1 gun ranging. Common shell 1000 yards," Peter called out the gunnery orders, which Hills repeated, to his crew. Peter then pointed out the most prominent sangars to both Sergeants.

"Number 1 gun, Fire."

"Fire!" echoed Hills. Bang! Re-echoed the screw gun. The 7-pound shell flew high and on line but it exploded short.

"Left Section 5 rounds Shrapnel 1200 yards. Independent targets, Fire." Fuse setters turned, rammers swung, cartridges were pierced and friction tubes pulled. Bang – Bang. The two screw guns started searching out the sangars and showering their occupants with a deadly hail of metal.

There was still that nullah though. Was it worth lobbing a few shells into it just in case? No, if the infantry commander saw the explosions in it he might assume that there was an actual danger there and feel obliged to send extra men to cover that flank.

The two screw guns had completed their fire order. Peter waited to allow the gun smoke to clear from the position, and from the target area. Most of the sangars were still occupied, as he expected, but those closest to the Highlanders seemed to be empty.

"Left section 10 rounds Shrapnel. Independent targets. Fire." Before a gun could fire, Peter called out to Sergeant Hills, "Sergeant, I'm going forward onto that large rock. Over there on our left front. I want to see if there are any tribesmen hiding in that nullah. This blasted gun smoke covers everything."

"That's very risky, sir, going near to them nullahs."

"Have no fear, Sergeant, I'll keep my eyes peeled."

"I'll send Digby, my Number 7 with you, sir. 'E's got a good pair of eyes."

"Alright. Send him on after me." Peter set off in a crouching run towards the large section of rock. When he reached it he stood upright under its cover and carefully scanned the surrounding areas, which was just broken and tumbled rock with open shale areas in between. In the middle distance the same rocks spread up the hillside past the opening of the wide mouth nullah but from his low position it was still not possible to see inside. Further up the hill, the tribesmen were cowering behind their sangars under the hail of Shrapnel – and about to face the Highlanders. Rather them than me, thought Peter.

"Gunner Digby reporting, sir. Sergeant Hills sent me."

"Right, Digby, follow me." The two men scrambled up the large tumbled rock which was no more than 30 feet high. Eventually Peter stood on the extreme top, while Digby stayed on a ledge just a few feet below.

"Keep an eye out for any movement around us, Digby," called Peter as he searched the area with his binoculars. He carefully examined the entrance of the nullah but still could not see far enough to be certain that it did not pose a danger to his guns or the infantry. He turned his glasses to the hill again and the Afghans. He then noticed a particularly well-concealed sangar; it was closer than he had expected and likely to flank the Highlanders' advance.

WEEERRR!

The sound of an incoming shell made him crouch but, being on the top of the rock, he was too exposed for this action to be of any use. There was a loud clunk and thud as the shell landed only twenty feet from the two men, showering them with rock splinters and shale. It was silent! The shell had failed to explode! Peter instantly stood upright. Where was that gun?

As he scanned the far rocks he heard a strangled gurgle come from Digby below him. The gunner was stretched out at the foot of the rock, his head lying in a pool of blood. Peter scrambled down to the wounded lad and gently turned him onto his back. A jagged rock splinter, thrown by the dud shell, had slashed a terrible wound into the youngster's neck and he was obviously beyond any help. Peter watched Digby's eyes gradually glaze as his lifeblood poured from the torn jugular to soak into the thin soil. Yet another life given for the Empire.

"Oh God," Peter lifted the gunner's hand, it was so young. "Oh God." He closed the dead boy's eyes. This gave some semblance of peace to the youngster as he lay in the pool of his own blood.

Peter quickly stood up and started looking again for the enemy gun. The dud shell had come from the hills, well over to the west. Any smoke from the first shot would have long dispersed but there was just the hope he could spot some movement as the enemy gunners went through the loading drill.

A great burst of white smoke appeared in Peter's view through his glasses. It must be the enemy gun firing again but it appeared to be a very large explosion for a single field gun As the smoke drifted away he could see, at the foot of the far hill 2000 yards away, a litter of white-clad bodies and a wheel canted at an angle. The Afghan gun had burst its barrel on firing, and was now lying on a smashed carriage with its gunners virtually wiped out to a man. Double cartridge loading in the excitement of battle was easily done; it was an error that was only overcome by strict training and many hours of practice.

Peter saw the Highlanders scrambling down the hillside, and he could see the tribesmen in the hidden sangar preparing to fire into the ranks of the Gordons.

He turned to run back to his guns when a large orange ball of fire appeared to his right. It knocked his legs from under him and threw him forward to sprawl onto the sand. An explosion roared around him but he felt no pain as he fell. His helmet spun off his head and rolled towards the large rock. There was still no pain, just a pressure on his chest and a slowly spinning sun.

He shook his head and felt the rush of blood in his mouth as it poured out mixed with saliva. His chest hurt now. He looked down and watched as the scarlet liquid slowly drained into the soil.

He knew then that he was dying; he was watching his own blood, pouring from his torn lungs, soak into the Afghan sand. It was the Mullah's curse come to fruition. That dud shell had exploded late, and sanctified an old religious man's wish.

He spat a large gob of blood onto the ground and saw part of a tooth lying in the dust mixed with the gore. Then gingerly, with finger and tongue, he examined his right cheek where he found that a metal or rock splinter had slashed in and removed some of his teeth.

I'm not dying! It is only a wound in my mouth. I must get back to the section at once. Lying on the sand he rolled over and looked at his legs which were numb and immovable, the left leg was covered in blood which was steadily seeping through his trousers, while the right leg had a gash high up on the inside thigh. But both of his arms were undamaged and, except for the pressure in his chest, he could breathe all right. Flopping onto his stomach he dug his elbows into the shale and pulled himself around the rock and started slowly to drag himself towards the guns.

The ground was flat and open but covered with the small rocks and shale, which quickly cut through his jacket and tore at his elbows. He could see, through the gun smoke, the two screw guns sending the shells smashing into the sangars. He wondered if anyone had seen his fall, and could they do anything if they had. The Highlanders needed the guns to cover their charge over the open ground against the well-defended sangars – so there was little time for the gunners to help the wounded. He dug his elbows in and, with the pain now starting to sear through his legs, he dragged himself forward a few more feet. He paused to rest and, looking towards the guns, saw a stocky figure sprinting towards him – he was side-stepping like a rugby fly half. Through the dust and smoke, Peter saw the figure of Sergeant Hills.

Peter noticed puffs of sand being kicked up around the running man and also in the space between them. Someone was firing at them from quite close behind. He rolled onto his side to look behind, and what he saw there turned his stomach to water.

A large group of tribesmen had belched out of the nullah, some were kneeling down and firing while the rest, a group of fifty or more were racing towards him. Oh God they mustn't get me! Peter's mind screamed at him. He rolled onto his stomach and scrambled at the shale with his arms trying to get nearer to the ducking, darting figure of Sergeant Hills.

Suddenly Hills fell full length onto the sand. He had been hit! He scrambled up with blood pouring from his right thigh. The section's guns behind him continued their intense barrage of Shrapnel but the screaming shells only brought assistance to the Highlanders – no help could be given to a Queen's officer and his brave Sergeant.

Peter looked over his shoulder and saw that the running tribesmen were only a couple of hundred yards away. Hills hobbled the last few yards and threw himself down beside Peter but facing away from him.

"Put your arms around me neck, sir," Hills called over his shoulder.

Peter obeyed; Hills rolled onto his stomach then slowly rose onto all fours, and eventually stood up with Peter on his back. "'Old on, sir," he grunted through clenched teeth then, with a groan he started to stumble towards the screw guns. Peter could hear the whirr of the bullets as the Afghans fired at the two of them as they slowly shuffled along. The running Afghans would easily catch them before Hills reached the gun position. Would it be a tearing slash of a tulwar to end it all quickly or would the two men be dragged away to provide hours of amusement while they screamed for their own death?

A stinging crack from the front told Peter that someone was using a Martini Henry. He looked towards the section and saw a figure clear of the smoke kneeling and firing. That would be Powell. He would be able to hit some of the pursuers but not many.

Hills tripped and fell onto his knees. Peter fell from his shoulders, the pain of his wounded legs hitting the ground made him cry out. Hills scrambled to his feet and roared out – "KEEP FIRING!"

Once more he lifted Peter onto his back and again staggered on with painfully slow steps.

Peter could see Number 1 gun bellow a cloud of smoke which, when it cleared, revealed the crew going through the loading process but the gun was being trained directly at himself and Hills. He saw the Number 3 inserting the cartridge and then the case shot. Hills's breathing sounded like coarse sandpaper on rough wood as he staggered onwards. The Number 2 deftly swung his rammer. Hills was lurching closer foot by foot but the running tribesmen were almost on him. Peter saw Number 5 place the friction tube in the vent – raise his hand and...

Sergeant Hills threw himself flat on his face, rolled onto his side and covered Peter's head with his body as Number 1 gun fired. Peter heard the scream of the 150 balls from the case shot tear through the air only three feet above him as they sped on their way to annihilate the pursuing Afghans. The howling spinning metal ripped into the leading warriors. Of the fifty who were in the chase the leading half were either dead or wounded. But they were only stopped fifty yards from the two wounded men.

"Pick the bones out of that," muttered Hills. "Come on, sir, arms around me neck, there's only a short way to go."

Chapter 20

Peter started to reach out across Hills's back, and then stopped.

"No, Sergeant, you've done your bit. Look over there, some of the lads're coming to get us."

Four of the drivers were running out from the gun site to help the two men. There was no imminent danger from the survivors of the chasing group but a very large number of Afghans had now swarmed out of the nullah and they threatened to swamp not only the gunners' position but also turn the flank of the unsuspecting Highlanders, who were halfway down the slope.

The first two drivers reached Peter and started to lift him by the shoulders, the other two arrived and caught hold of Hills who shrugged them off. "Four of you carry Lieutenant Rutland. Careful now, 'es not very fit, 'is legs is bad."

The group of gunners scrambled back to the gun position knowing full well that the mass of tribesmen were charging down on them and that neither of the screw guns could fire while they obstructed the line of fire. As they arrived at the guns Sergeant Farrant yelled out, "'Ere they come again!"

The drivers laid Peter down leaning against a rock behind the guns. Sergeant Hills knelt down beside him and said, "Shall I take over, sir?"

"No, Sergeant. Continue firing case shot and reversed Shrapnel but detach the restraining ropes from the gun wheels. We'll retreat with the recoil back into the valley, it'll give us a bit more distance." Hills stood up with a grimace as the pain in his thigh cut into him. With a bloody rag in his clenched fist pushed hard against his thigh, he called to

Sergeant Farrant and then staggered over to his gun to explain to Bombardier Smith the unusual drill.

"Driver!" Peter called out to a man who was standing, twenty yards behind the ready ammunition, holding three mules by their head collars. "Bring those mules over here." One of the animals with its empty carrying harness would be ideal to help Peter to stand and move, if only he can hang on.

"Help me up to catch hold of the harness." The driver manoeuvred the mules in front of Peter then he bent down, put his hand into Peter's Sam Browne belt and lifted him up bodily. Peter managed to catch hold of the wheel cradles on the harness and heave his body up so that his damaged legs dangled beside the mule. The agony of his wounds screamed at him but at least he could now move.

"Lead him back to that rock over there," he grunted. The pain in his legs was now a searing throb, yet he could feel the blood trickling down into his boots. Slowly the driver turned the mule and led it back thirty yards behind the guns. Peter screwed up his eyes with the agony as the animal jolted his wounds at almost every stride.

"Stop here," Peter ordered. "Now help me down. I want to sit in front of this boulder."

The driver caught hold of Peter's belt. "Put yer arm around me neck, sir, and I can lower yer down, slowly like." Peter did as he was instructed and felt himself lifted bodily by the waist then lowered to the ground. Then the driver stood astride him and with his arms under Peter's armpits sat him against the large boulder. "I'll get yer some morphine to kill the pain in yer legs."

"No," ordered Peter through clenched teeth. "It'll make me unconscious."

"No it won't, sir. I've seen it before on wounded men. They're wide-awake and sensible but their wounds don't hurt. Makes yer eyeballs go to pinpricks though."

"My eyeballs go to pinpricks? What on earth do you mean?" queried Peter, his hand held against his torn cheek. The wounds in his legs were agony.

"Not yer actual eyes, just the bit in the middle."

"Oh the iris. Alright, see if you can get me a small dose," he gasped.

The driver ran over to a medical orderly who was attending to a wounded gunner lying just behind the guns. The orderly rose from his patient and ran across to Peter. He started to pull the bloodstained cloth from the wounded legs but Peter brushed his hands away. "Just give me something that'll kill the pain then go back to the wounded," Peter ordered.

The orderly rummaged in his bag and pulled out a small glass bottle filled with a clear liquid, he uncorked it and held the bottle up to Peter's lips. "It won't make me unconscious will it?" Peter asked.

"No, sir, just drink half now and the rest in an hour's time – if we're still here that is."

Peter held the bottle to his lips and let a spoonful of morphine slip into his mouth; that was about half the contents. He swallowed the tasteless liquid and then waved the orderly away, sending him back to his work. He pushed the cork back into the bottle and put it down beside him, for use later on – if we are here that is.

The screw guns were pounding away; though Peter could see little of the charging Afghans, he could tell by the fury with which the two Sergeants drove their men that the hordes were not far away.

A clatter of shod hooves on the rocky surface behind made Peter turn his head. A horse cantered past the boulder; its rider vaulted from the saddle and ran the last few yards towards Number 1 gun. It was Gunner Hamblin, and he had brought back Dainby's horse.

Gunner Jones, the Number 5, was standing beside the gun preparing a friction tube when a bullet hit him high in the chest. He spun round with a grunt and fell face downwards onto the ground. Hamblin sprinted the last few yards then stopped and grabbed the wounded Number 5, turned him over and dragged him a few feet from the gun. Hamblin undid the man's belt, pulled off the friction tube case, grabbed the lanyard and ran back to the gun. He placed the tube into the vent, fixed the lanyard and pulled. The gunpowder charge exploded, throwing the spinning shell splinters into the ever nearer charging Afghan masses.

It was during this few seconds' pause that, as the smoke cleared, Peter could see that the tribesmen were charging in waves; the front men were shooting while the others advanced. The Afghan Snider and Enfield rifle bullets were slamming into the gunners who had no shield or rock cover to protect them. To the right of the gun position, higher up the slope Peter could now see that a large group of Highlanders had swung left to meet this surprise attack but it was obvious that unless they flew, they could not reach the guns in time.

"Drivers!" yelled Peter at the top of his voice. "Leave the mules. Use spare carbines at once." He waved his arms to attract their attention. "All of you. NOW! Leave the mules." Some of the drivers knotted the collar ropes of their animals together, while others just grabbed a carbine and ran to the battle line, and started shooting straight away. That gave another fifteen riflemen to support the gunners, it might just be enough. Enough to buy us a few seconds, a few seconds to get the Gordons those few precious yards closer.

Peter looked round, what else could be done? At each explosion from the screw guns they recoiled back four or five feet but the gunners were still well out of the rocky valley. The Highlanders were now charging down the hill screaming their war cry. But it looked as though the tribesmen would reach the guns first. In fact some of them might have outflanked the position already. It was so difficult to tell in all this smoke.

Peter was all alone among the tied mules. His section was fighting for their lives just thirty yards away. His legs felt numb; the morphine had done the trick. The cacophonous noise of the pounding charges, the rifle shots and the ricocheting bullets were all enveloping. Then he saw three Afghans creeping through the boulders to the left of the section beyond the drivers.

"Watch your left flank!" he yelled. "Enemy on the left flank." He screamed out the warning but no one could hear him. The three Afghans would simply shoot his men in enfilade and they would never know. Peter tugged at his holster and pulled out his heavy Enfield revolver. Holding it very carefully with both hands on the butt, he fired once, twice, three times. One of the warriors spun round, a revolver bullet had struck him in the leg. Peter fired again and again. Then one of the drivers turned and, seeing the danger, yelled to his neighbour and they both started firing at this extra hazard. Peter fired his last round at the two tribesmen who had either hidden or been hit by the drivers.

A gunner was running back towards the mules. It was Gunner Mabbs. "What do you want, Gunner?"

"More carbine ammo', sir." He was frantically pulling at an ammunition box on the mule carrier. He jerked out a number of packets of ammunition, and sprinted back to the guns and the smoke. Peter could still hear the screams of the Afghans as they closed but he could also hear the roar of the Highlanders as they charged down the slope, getting closer – but would they be in time?

It was at that moment that he heard a deep laugh.

"Ha ha." The sound was so out of place that he disbelieved his senses.

A laugh? Impossible!

"At last, Rutlandi," boomed a deep voice. Peter jerked his head round and saw the large figure of a turbaned tribesman.

It was Badal! The man he had shot when rescuing Bee, the man who had murdered poor Assan. He was pushing his way past the tied mules near to Dainby's horse. He must have crept in with the other three tribesmen then swung round behind the section until he saw Peter lying alone, away from the guns, ready to be slain. Badal was a man prepared to sacrifice anything just to be able to kill one special man, and here was his victim ready for sacrifice.

Slowly he walked towards Peter, just like the last meeting, with a tulwar sword in his hand but this time it was held low with the point held towards his victim. Peter lifted his revolver, aimed carefully at the large chest, and fired.

Click! All six rounds had been fired at the three Afghan warriors. The empty heavy Enfield was just so much scrap metal. His spare ammunition pouch was on his belt behind him but the rounds were always difficult to extract even under normal conditions. He half rolled onto his side and groped with his left hand at the buckled flap. Badal slowly approached, the confident smile on his lips.

Peter felt the flap buckle come undone and he flipped back the lid; he could feel the cartridge rims in their separate compartments. Blindly he tried to get his nail under the rim. Just one – that was all he wanted!

"My father's curse on your family has come at last oh Angrezi infidel. A thousand pities that your death cannot be slow but it will certainly be painful. Allah is generous." The screw guns boomed; the smoke swirled; the Highlanders and the Afghans screamed – but Badal and Peter were all alone and about to join in a deadly embrace.

At last! One cartridge lifted up; with finger and thumb Peter pulled it clear. He brought it round to place it in the revolver but his morphined brain failed him for a split second. His numbed fingers allowed the precious bullet to fall behind him out of sight. He scrambled his hand over the sand but only succeeded in burying the life-saving cartridge. There was no time to try for another.

"At last, Rutlandi," repeated Badal. "You thought my father's Koran would save you but it only saves true believers," the deep voice pronounced.

Badal was only ten feet away; he raised the tulwar above his head ready to sweep it down on this accursed infidel. Peter watched hoping that he could deflect the cutting blade with the empty revolver then maybe grapple with Badal's sword arm. The Afghan was savouring the moment of pure revenge. His deep voice boomed as, holding the raised sword on high, he pronounced. "Your death is here. Now, go slowly to meet thy Go—"

A look of shock slapped across his face! He staggered and looked down at the bloody Artillery bayonet that was protruding from the centre of his chest. It had entered between his back ribs alongside his spine. For a second Badal stood, feet apart, looking at this monstrous piece of bloody steel, then he crashed forward, like a felled tree, his head striking the ground at Peter's feet.

"Blimey, sir, that was close." Gunner Mabbs was standing over Badal, tugging at the bayonet that was still attached to his carbine. "You orlright?"

"Yes, Mabbs," gasped Peter, "Thank you – you saved my life."

"Jus' came back for more ammo'. Gotta dash. Bleedin' baby's still crying." The cockney humour never failed, it was still there even when right on the edge of the Pit. The gunner grabbed more packets from the ammunition box and ran back to the streaming smoke and the noise of battle.

Peter looked down at Badal's face. The look of utter astonishment was still etched in the dead eyes. The silent mouth remained open as though trying to complete his speech of vengeance that was surely his. Badal's spirit may well be on its way to an Islamic paradise to worship his God, but his earthly remains were still in a state of shock at being unable to complete its function of slaying the accursed Rutlandi.

A swirl of moving air gently spread dust onto the dead eyes; at the same time it pushed away the blanket of smoke that had lain over the screw guns. The terrible scene was almost a blur of colour and action. The Highlanders had arrived at the gunners' position within seconds of the Afghans, and right now a scrambling melee of tribesmen, gunners and Highlanders were heaving around – hacking, stabbing, wounding and dying. Another group of charging Gordons slammed into the battle, then slowly but with a growing momentum the surging force started to move away from the guns.

The tribesmen had not overrun the position but neither were they retreating. They were going to win or die fighting, and this they did. These warriors knew that their cause was right and just, it had the blessing of Allah, it was a holy war. They did not ask for quarter nor did they give any, so they died to a man; not one of them ran from the bloody field. Even when they were wounded they continued to fight with sword and dagger until they joined the other Mujaheddin in Paradise as they sat at the feet of their God.

Eventually the action stilled as the Afghans died. The weary gunners staggered to help their wounded. The smoke from the guns had long drifted away so that Peter had been able to watch the final scene of this most horrible play before him. He sat alone, yet right on the edge of the conflict, while at his feet lay the man who was to have been the avenger but Badal was ended, in flesh and in spirit. It was over.

Peter's legs were now throbbing and the sharp pains were starting to return. He stretched out his hand to the small glass bottle lying beside him on its side. He picked it up – but it was empty; the precious painkiller had drained out of the cork that he had fitted too loosely. He could not ask the orderlies for more, they were too busy with the other wounded, and they would certainly need all the available morphine for the men who were suffering greater pain than his.

A tall figure appeared from out of the mass. "Peter, are you badly hurt?" It was the welcome Scottish voice of Angus Hamilton, who knelt down beside him.

"No I'm alright now, thank you, Angus," Peter replied wearily. "Your men arrived just in the nick of time. We all owe our lives to you."

"Your legs look bad. I'll get a medical orderly to bandage you up."

"No, Angus, there's no need. They gave me some morphine so I'm not in any pain. They must treat the seriously wounded first. I'd be grateful though if you could find one of my Sergeants for me. I hope that at least one of them's alive."

"Certainly I'll go at once." Angus stood up and looked around him. "Sergeant MacKay!" he shouted to a massive kilted figure some distance away. "I want one of your medical orderlies for this officer at once." Then ignoring Peter's protests he strode towards the guns in search of the Section sergeants.

Peter could feel the pain in his legs starting again to tear into him but he noticed that the blood was no longer seeping out of his trousers. He presumed that was good news; how much blood he had lost he did not know but it was now difficult to concentrate – even to focus his eyes. The mules standing near to him appeared hazy, and their legs seemed to wobble in the middle.

A squat hobbling figure emerged from the distant haze of Peter's sight. It was Sergeant Hills with two gunners and a Scottish medical orderly. The Highlander immediately pulled a bottle out of his medical pack, removed the cork and pressed it to Peter's mouth. The burning liquid cascaded over his tongue, hit his torn cheek and teeth then swirled down his throat in a number of gulps. It was neat whisky! My God, he thought if the Afghans don't kill me, then the Scots surely will.

A stretcher was laid alongside of him and the orderly and the two gunners lifted him onto it. He groaned involuntarily at the pain caused while his legs were held and moved.

"For Christ's sake," barked Hills, "be careful, you clumsy buggers!"

As Peter felt himself carried on the stretcher he tried to wipe the pain from his mind by enlarging on the thought that had just entered his mind. "I've never heard Hills swear before." Under the greatest provocation from the most stupid of recruits, Hills had never been known to swear.

"Sergeant," he croaked through the enveloping drowsiness. "What about the Section?"

"Don't you worry, sir. The Gordons've taken the position. We've been told to withdraw. Centre Section's on its way to give the 'ighlanders support for the attack. You just rest while they carry you back to the Field Hospital."

Peter tried to ask who had been killed but the words would not move from his brain to his lips. He badly wanted to know, for the section must be in a bad way if they are being relieved. Everything now was blurring. He felt so tired, his head lolled to the side, and with great difficulty he straightened it up to peer with myopic eyes at the rest of the section who were forming up. The crunch of their boots on the rocks grew fainter, leaving just the nagging thought, as the dark curtain swept over him – strange that Hills should swear.

Chapter 21

Ayub Khan had been defeated. He had fled the field leaving his artillery, ammunition, baggage and the majority of his army. His own bodyguard still guarded his royal person but he was a hunted fugitive. The dedicated Mujaheddin section of his army fought on, and they died fighting but the majority of his soldiers, who were simple peasant tribesmen just faded into the hills as the tide of battle turned against them. Eventually they returned to their own villages weeks, sometimes months, later having travelled many miles to continue their existence of ploughing and harvesting.

Even while the battle was being fought the withdrawal of the British Army from Afghanistan was being decided in Westminster. The Government knew that though the Army could win pitched battles against the Afghans, the tribesmen could never be subjugated. Better to withdraw when you are on top, rather than retreat later with your tail between your legs. India was now safe from Russian expansionism.

Immediately after the battle, the Field Hospital had commandeered a large white painted, mud brick house on the edge of Deh-I-Khoja. This spacious dwelling was quickly filled up with the wounded of the British contingent who, during the next few days, sorted themselves into three distinct groups. Those who were seriously wounded mostly died, leaving only a few to be nursed back to health; the lightly wounded members had by now mainly returned to their units, well bandaged up but mobile; the third group were those who were incapacitated, still needed nursing and had managed to stay alive.

Peter was in this last group, having been rescued, then cleaned up and finally stitched up. Sergeant Hills was in the middle group who, ten days after the battle, still reported to the hospital for the doctors to change their dressing and examine their wounds.

"Sergeant Hills. Keep still! Your precious section can manage without you for another ten minutes while I finish dressing this wound." Beatrice Nashton spoke with an authoritative voice so, obediently, Sergeant Hills lay motionless and waited. He felt discomfort, not from the wound, but from the fact that he was lying on a bed without his trousers on, in front of a lady.

Bee had removed the old dressing from the wound on his thigh, then she had prodded it and probed it and even smelled it.

"Yes, that's healing nicely. No sign of gangrene or pustulence, just good old scar tissue. You shouldn't be walking on it really but I doubt if even Bobs could make you stay in bed."

"I'll be alright, Miss."

Bee smiled, "I'm sure you will, Sergeant, you're probably indestructible." She placed a clean pad on the wound and then carefully and neatly bandaged the upper part of his leg. Finally she knotted the bandage ends and tucked them in.

"There you are, Sergeant. You can put your trousers back on now."

"Thank you, Miss. I'm very grateful to you for all you've done." He quickly adjusted his uniform and added, "We all are. You're our angel."

Bee had been standing with her back to him while he dressed. Now she turned towards him with a smile on her face. Hills was standing by the doorway, helmet under his arm waiting to be dismissed. She walked over to him and to his utter amazement, gave him a kiss on his cheek.

"That, Sergeant, is to thank you for saving Mr Rutland's life. I've heard all about your brave action, without it he would certainly have died.

"Oh I don't know about that, Miss."

"Well I do. And so does every one else – even Bobs knows." She burst out laughing at his reaction, for Hills was actually standing there with his mouth open, amazed at the idea of Bobs being told of anything to do with a mere Sergeant.

Bee paused in her laughter and explained, "When Major Tenet received the full report from Mr Rutland, he passed it on to the General – so even he knows."

Hills recovered his composure and asked, "'Ow is Lieutenant Rutland, Miss?"

"Very weak. He nearly bled to death but the Surgeon has stitched up his legs and it's now just a matter of time and rest. He'll pull through; you gunners seem to be very tough."

"Could I go and see 'im? The men 'ave asked 'ow 'e is."

"Yes of course you can but mind, only for a few minutes. Through that door over there but if he's still asleep don't wake him, he needs lots of rest."

"Thank you, Miss, I'll only stay a minute," Hills promised. He left the surgery and walked down the corridor to a green painted door. Gently he lifted the latch and slowly opened the door. The room was very dim with the shutters closed but the air inside was cool and sweet. On large bed, covered with an Army sheet, lay Peter. His face was a sallow white colour against the pillow. His eyes were open and he smiled as he recognised Hills. "Come in, Sergeant," he called, "It's good to see you again. How's your leg?"

"Almost better now thank you, sir, Miss Nashton 'as just changed the dressing. 'ow are you, sir?"

"As weak as a kitten, and bored out of my mind. Major Tenet called in the other day and I was able to make a report to him. He knows how you saved my life and commanded the section. We're very proud of you, Sergeant."

"Thank you, sir." Hills stared at the blank wall behind Peter. "The men wanted to know 'ow you was coming along, sir." Peter smiled at the subtle change of subject, then he asked, "Have you spoken to Hamblin about his disappearance?"

"Yes sir, 'e'd gone after the Captain's 'orse as we thought, and 'e rejoined the section just before tribesmen 'it us." Hills paused. "I suppose you'll want to see 'im, sir; 'e fought like a lion though." Peter acknowledged Hill's character reference for Hamblin but both men knew that the rescue of a horse was no excuse for absenting himself like that, especially at such a crucial time, just before a battle.

"I'll see him tomorrow afternoon. Put him on a charge of Absent Without Leave; it should be Desertion in the face of the enemy in fact." Peter reached across to the table beside his bed and picked up a writing pad. He opened it and took out a piece of paper that was tucked inside.

"Sergeant, I want you to find out the answers to these questions for me." He handed the note to Hills. "I'd like to have all the answers before midday tomorrow if you can manage it."

Captain Toby Warburton lounged in a chair beside Peter's bed. "Edward Anstruther's death was a great tragedy," he said, "No Englishman understood the Afghan race better. His actions did more for reconciliation and peace between the races than anyone will ever know. I have at last found the group of Ayatollahs who Edward wanted to have your Koran."

"Is it that important?" asked Peter.

"Without doubt. Its return will consolidate a large group of nationalistic and realistic chiefs who will certainly strive for a peaceful settlement."

"You mean that it will make it easier to incorporate Afghanistan into the Empire and subjugate its people." Peter felt very uneasy.

"Good Lord no!" exclaimed Toby. "We're not staying here."

"You mean we've fought this bloody war just to leave the country. It was all for nothing?"

Warburton sat up straight in his chair. "You've got it all wrong. We invaded Afghanistan to keep the Russians out. If we hadn't they would have been into India within a year. No we aren't staying here because it is obvious that this is not a country that anyone can conquer and subjugate. Any power, now or in the future, who feel the need to suppress the Afghans is in for a bad time and a bloody nose. History proves it."

He stood up. "I mustn't keep you from your rest anymore. Your father's Koran is going back to where it belongs. And honestly the sooner you are out of Afghanistan the better. You are, to say the least, not popular with the natives."

The sound of marching feet in the corridor could be clearly heard. They seemed to stop outside the door leading to Peter's room.

"What on earth is that?" asked Warburton.

"I expect it is Sergeant Hills with a gunner on a charge to see me."

"I'll leave you then. It is ironic that you should arrive here with a religious relic, namely the Koran, and leave with another relic – namely the tulwar."

"Do you think I should return that as well"?

"Certainly not. You keep the damned thing – safely in England. Goodbye, Peter."

"Goodbye, Toby." The door opened and Sergeant Hills entered the room just as Captain Warburton was leaving.

"Gunner 'amblin on Section Commander's report, sir."

"Bring him in, Sergeant," Peter instructed.

"Prisoner and escort." Hills quietly ordered, "Quick march. Left. Right. Left. Right. Left. Right. 'alt. Right turn." The three men, with Hamblin in the centre halted at the foot of Peter's bed, then turned to face him.

"Gunner 'amblin, sir," reported Hills. "Charged that on September 1st 1880 did go absent without leave for a period of two hours."

Peter looked at the gunner. "Gunner Hamblin, how do you plead, guilty or not guilty?"

"Guilty, sir," replied Hamblin.

"Will you accept my decision or do you want to appear before the Battery Commander?"

"I'll take your decision, sir."

"Do you have anything to say before I give punishment?"

"No, sir. Nothing to say."

"Hamblin you are aware that you did a very foolish act. You endangered your own life and prejudiced the safety of the section by your absence. All this was to save just one horse. This type of act must never, I say again, never be repeated. Do you understand?"

"Yes, sir."

"You will be fined £10, to be deducted from your pay or savings."

Hamblin's mouth dropped open. £10! That was an enormous amount. At one shilling a day he only earned £18 and 4 shillings a year, and that was before stoppages for uniform, food etc. He would never be able to pay off such a massive fine; he was broken.

"Prisoner and escort, right turn," ordered Hills, "Quick march." He held the door open to allow the three men to march into the corridor.

"'Alt!"

"Sergeant Hills," Peter called, "Dismiss the escort and send Hamblin in to me please."

"Certainly, sir," Hills turned towards the three men. "Prisoner and escort – dismiss. 'Amblin, report to Lieutenant Rutland."

The gunner again marched into the room, halted at the foot of the bed, and saluted.

"Gunner Hamblin reporting, sir," Sergeant Hills also returned to the room, closed the door and stood beside Peter's bed, at attention.

"Sergeant, did you get the answers to my questions I asked yesterday?"

"Yes, sir. They're written down 'ere, sir."

He took a sheet of paper from his tunic pocket and handed it to Peter who read it at some length and then he addressed the gunner.

"Hamblin, the incident of your absence on 1st September is now closed, though I hope not forgotten by you. There is however one small matter to be cleared up." Peter referred to the sheet of paper, "and that is Captain Dainby's horse. Sergeant Hills has enquired of the Quartermaster's section if there is a purchase value on the animal and recovered equipment. The QM informs him that the standing rate for a horse and saddlery, recovered in good condition, is –" he looked at the paper and read out "– thirty-seven pounds nine shillings and sixpence."

Hamblin was looking at Peter with bewilderment on his face. From the disaster of a few minutes ago, his prospects now seemed to have completely changed, though he was obviously not absolutely certain yet.

"This means that after the deduction of your fine of ten pounds, there is still an amount owing to you of twenty-seven pounds, nine shillings and six pence." The amazed gunner could hardly believe his ears. It seemed to be true.

"For me, sir?" he queried.

"For you Gunner," Peter replied. "You can have all the money within the next seven days or it can be put into safe keeping for your return to England."

"Thank you very much, sir," beamed Hamblin. "Can I have the nine and a tanner now and the rest to be 'eld for me?"

"A very wise decision. As soon as the money is available Sergeant Hills will inform you." Peter looked up at Hills. "That's all thank you, Sergeant."

"Gunner 'amblin. Dismiss," ordered Hills. The gunner saluted, turned and marched out still with a broad grin on his face; he was closely followed by his sergeant. When they were both in the corridor and the door to Peter's room was closed, Hills spoke quietly to the gunner.

"Listen, my lad, never try anything like that again. Saving an 'orse indeed." Hills snorted in disgust. "You could've faced a flogging for desertion or even worse. Also most officers would 'ave kept the QM's purchase money for themselves, as Lieutenant Rutland was fully entitled to do. So remember, you've used up all your issue of luck for this year – and probably even next."

"Right, Sarn't. I won't let you or the Lieutenant down."

"Hmph," grunted Hills, then both men marched back to their billets.

Though Peter felt weak as he recuperated, he also found that time hung very heavily as the days dragged slowly by. Bee spent many of her evenings with him but during the day he was generally alone. He ate well, slept well and even tried some exercises with his arms in an attempt to strengthen himself but he was not even allowed to try walking. The Surgeon Major was satisfied that his wounds were closing nicely and except for the scars he would be able to walk, run and ride once he had regained his strength.

One afternoon Peter was lying down feeling drowsy when the door opened and Bee entered the room. "What a lovely surprise," he beamed. "Couldn't you wait until this evening?"

She bent over the bed and kissed him. "I've got some news for you."

"From the look on your face it must be good news."

"It is," she paused then sat on the edge of the bed and held his hand. "We're going home."

"What! Home? When? Both of us? How?"

"Which question do you want answered first," she laughed and squeezed his hand.

"All of them. Now what is this all about?"

"Well," she started, "Surgeon Major Sharp has just told me that a column is returning to Quetta taking with them all the wounded who can travel by ambulance, and they're to be invalided home on a ship leaving Karachi. You're one of the lucky ones." She paused and looked down at their joined hands. "I've been asked to act as a medical orderly for the column so I'll be travelling with you."

"That's marvellous, darling, that means we will be going home together." Peter was delighted but he saw that Bee was still looking at their hands. She did not seem to be as overjoyed as he felt.

"Is anything wrong?" he asked. "We're going home."

"Peter you are going home. I'm going to England. I have no home. I have an Aunt in Yorkshire who I saw fifteen years ago, other than that I've always been with my father or here in India." Peter raised his hand and gently touched her cheek.

"Darling, your home's going to be with me, because I love you."

She tilted her head against his hand. "Will our love last in England, or is it only here in Afghanistan, where we found it?"

"Don't be silly," he murmured. "It'll be a world-wide love, knowing no boundaries." He gently pulled her towards him and kissed her.

"I will love you everywhere." Again they kissed.

"Even in Yorkshire?" she asked.

"Even in Yorkshire."

Historical Note

2.5 inch Rifled Muzzle Loading (RML) Mountain Gun "The Screw Gun."

This mountain gun was based on a new system invented by Colonel Le Mesurier in 1876. A new gunpowder had been invented but a barrel that was able to use it had to be longer, and so heavier. While the carriage and wheels were carried in their parts by mules as usual, the new system was to have the barrel in two parts, each of one mule load. These were joined by a trunnion ring attached to the muzzle section which allowed it to be 'screwed' to the breech section. The completed barrel length was 66.5 ins. The shell weighed 7lbs. Currently, one of these guns is on show at Firepower the Royal Artillery Museum at Woolwich.

The mule gun train consisted of five mules, the first two mules for each part of the barrel, a third for the wheels, a forth for the carriage and the fifth for the other parts (elevating gear, axletree etc.)

This versatile gun was the standard equipment for mountain artillery from 1878 until after the Boer War, and was considered for many years to be the best mountain gun in the world. It caught the imagination of the British Press who named it the 'Screw Gun'. Rudyard Kipling then immortalised it in his famous poem 'The Screw Guns' which perfectly captures the atmosphere of the mule train high in the mountains.

It was first used in a mountain battery similar to Peter Rutland's in the Afghan War of 1878-80, which was the first of his many military adventures.

*More historical notes will be added to
www.roger-carpenter.co.uk

"The Screw Gun."

Breinigsville, PA USA
20 November 2009
227939BV00001B/11/P